# OPERATION TOMAHAWK

## NINJANS 4

Dave Kwan

# DISCLAIMER



Book Front Cover Credit: Artwork by LAYW - Adobe Stock

File#: 255401894   JPEG   3456 x 5184px

Book Back Cover Credit: Artwork by Dimitry Ersler - Adobe Stock

File#: 35604118   JPEG   3000 x 2000px



ISBN:
ISBN-13: 9781777310820

# DEDICATION

This book is dedicated
in honour and memory of
**Joe King**.
Frederick Joseph King.

When I was a kid swimming
at the local dam in Tweed, Ontario;
I fell and broke my arm
and repeatedly went under the water.
A young man named Joe King,
dove in and saved me from drowning.
I am alive today and very grateful
he was there to rescue me!

# ACKNOWLEDGEMENTS

With regards to online research
and finding helpful information,
The author wishes to acknowledge
the following sources:

Americanspecialops.com

Globalsecurity.org

GoArmy.com

Google.com

Military.com

Specialops.org

Wikipedia.org

YouTube.com

# CHAPTER ONE

*Trained By A Ninjan Master*

*Tommy stands sweaty and tired*

Tommy stands sweaty and tired, his lungs panting for air. Beads of perspiration trickle down his brow and muscular frame. On the top of a grassy knoll, two figures face each other with steel blades extended. The wind blows strands of Tommy's long hair across his face, he clears it away. Tommy holds the glossy black Katana poised for battle. His eyes dart to and fro, as his opponent moves from side to side. Tommy's Ninjan senses kick-in, there's a blur of flashing steel and he lifts his sword just in time to stop a ferocious sword attack. CLANG! Tommy pivots his foot and steps back in anticipation of his opponent's next move. As the opponent powerfully swings from the right side, Tommy drops his sword to deflect the blow - CLANG! Suddenly, Tommy lunges forward spinning his sword - his blade stops a quarter inch from the attacker's neck. His opponent freezes — then smiles! The man raises the fingers of his left hand to cautiously move Tommy's blade away from the neck.

Tommy lowers his weapon and remarks, "You almost had me, Grandpa!" Carl Long Grass, Tommy's Grandfather and Ninjan Master, replies with a delight, "Your sword technique has greatly improved! I would have beat you a year ago - but not now!" Tommy grins in response, "That's because of your great teaching Grandpa!" Carl puts his arm around his grandson with a fond hug, "My heart is proud you've become so skilled - a true Ninjan Warrior!" As the two walk together toward their vehicle parked near the pines, Tommy looks over with a whimsical expression, "Say, isn't it your turn to buy?" Carl stops mid-stride with a quick ponder, then shrugs with a slight groan, "Oh! You know, you're right! My treat this time,(eyes Tommy), where do you want to eat? Tommy's eyes light up as he blurts out, "Big Jack's

Roadhouse! I love their ribs and burgers!" Carl grins and nods as the Grandfather and Grandson walk toward the Ford Bronco.

Heading toward town, Carl and Tommy bounce and jostle about as the Bronco motors along the bumpy dirt road that cuts a rugged path through the wilderness. Tommy looks over at his Grandfather with a respectful gaze. His mind recalls outstanding moments from the past five years where Carl instructed Tommy in various Ninjan techniques. The young man stares at the trees, brush, and tall grass that sweep by, his memories are so vivid, so special! Tommy recalls being a scrawny sixteen-year old when he started his Ninjan training. During the past five years, Carl infused Tommy with Martial Arts training and Ninjan techniques. Tommy has turned into a strong muscular twenty-year old with lightning cat-like reflexes and Ninjan ability well beyond his years. Tommy closes his eyes and sees himself throwing the Shuriken, the sharp pointed metal stars sinking deep into their target. He handles the Ninjato and Katana swords with prowess and power - spinning, twirling, chopping, slicing and stabbing with lethal ability. In his mind's eye, he recalls how his Grandfather taught him to shoot the black arrows from the Ninjan bow to accurately hit targets. Tommy grins as he thinks back to times when he battled Carl in hand-to-hand combat; and the many times his Ninjan Master out-fought and out-maneuvered him, leaving him with important Ninjan lessons from the 'School-of-Hard-Knocks'. Those Combat techniques and lessons became etched into his repertoire of Ninjan skills.

The narrow dirt trail they trace back has now taken them to a gravel County Road. Carl turns the Bronco right and heads in the direction of town, toward the gastronomic destination of honey-glazed ribs and a mouth-watering Roadhouse Burger, topped with Monterey Jack cheese, crispy onion rings, sautéed mushrooms, tasty coleslaw, and sweet pickles.

In no time, the Ford Bronco reaches the blacktop highway that leads toward town. Carl slows down at the stop sign, idles the engine as he checks both directions. He signals and turns left, moving the Bronco onto the tarmac road toward Big Jack's Roadhouse, located a few miles on the outskirts of town. Carl glances at Tommy and remarks, "Your cousin Jody is doing pretty good in her Ninjan training! She has a ways to go - but soon, she'll catch up to you." Tommy smiles, "Jody's always been athletic and great at sports. The moment I heard you were going to train her - I knew she'd be a great student." The Grandfather proudly remarks, "She'll finish College in two years. Think I'll plan something to celebrate!" Tommy looks over as he responds, "Surprise her with something special! She'd love that! (He muses) Maybe a fancy dinner somewhere!" Carl grins, "A fancy dinner! Thanks Tommy! Yes Siree, a fancy dinner it'll be!" Up in the distance, they both see the big sign announcing Big Jack's Roadhouse. Carl slows the Bronco down, turns off the highway, and steers into the parking lot. People seem hungry today because the parking lot appears full. He sees an empty spot at the end of a row of vehicles and eases the Bronco into place, then cuts the engine. Tommy and Carl exit and walk toward the front entrance. Tommy turns to Carl with a smile and takes a big whiff, "Smell that BBQ!" Carl shakes his head with a grin and comments, "That should be a required Ninjan skill! Tommy remarks, "What skill?" Carl laughs and replies, "Having a nose for good food!" Both chuckle as they enter inside Big Jack's Roadhouse.

# CHAPTER TWO

*New Direction For A Young Man*

Carl glances at his grandson as they eat supper at the dining table. His grandson has been unusually quiet, seemingly lost in thought. The old man senses there's something stirring in Tommy's soul - a 'Coming-of-Age' restlessness that whirls around inside every young person as they ponder their next 'Big Step' in Life. Carl lifts the jug and pours himself a fresh glass of juice, then asks, "Tommy, you're really quiet - Is there something bothering you?" Tommy puts down his fork and moves his half-eaten plate to the side, and replies, "Grandpa, I've been thinking about what to do next? I finished High School two years ago - now that I'm turning 21, I've been wondering what to do with my life?" Carl takes a sip of juice and remarks, "Barry tells me you're doing real good and you'll make a fine Mechanic! He said you're more than welcome to stay on at his Auto Shop." Tommy smiles at learning of his boss's opinion. The young man stretches his legs, tilts his chair back a bit and comments, "I like working around cars and trucks - for that matter, any kind of vehicle! And Barry's been a good boss and pays me well. (stares off) But, inside I'm kinda restless, feeling like I need to leave Venture and the Indian Reserve, get out and see more of the world - do something different!" The grandfather looks tenderly at his grandson, "Tommy, soon you'll be old enough to leave. The Court said when you turn 21 you're free to leave - that's in three months. (tender gaze) Tommy, whatever you decide to do - stay or leave - you got my full support!" Tommy glances over and remarks with a big smile, "Thanks Grandpa! I know I got you in my corner!" The old man replies, "I'm there for you, son. - Always will be!"

Three months pass…

* * *

Sarah, Tommy's girlfriend of the past five years, is decorating the house interior with colourful streamers and balloons to celebrate Tommy's 21st Birthday. Her mom baked a long rectangular three-layer chocolate fudge cake for the special occasion. The top features a Katana sword done in icing with the words - "Happy Birthday Tommy". Carl comes out of his bedroom carrying a present wrapped with a big red bow. He places it on a side table and begins to help Sarah hang the streamers and balloons. HONK! HONK! Carl and Sarah go to the living room window to see who's there. Three cars, two pickups, and a minivan have just pulled into the driveway. Sarah rushes to open the front door and yells out, "You can park your cars out back behind the house!" The drivers nod and the vehicles drive around the house to disappear out of sight. Tommy's friends, fellow alumni from Gold Eagle, and some coworkers exit with presents in hand and walk around to the front entrance. Sarah opens the front door and stands to the side as people come inside. The entrance gets filled with smiles and hugs as everyone greets Sarah and Carl. Sarah announces, "Thanks for coming! (She points) You can put your presents on the side table." The guys and gals deposit their gifts on the table and begin to find a place to sit. One young lady looks around and asks, "Sarah, do you need help with the decorations?" Sarah replies with a smile, "Thanks for asking, but Carl and I are just finishing up." As the visitors get comfortable on the sofa and chairs, Carl and Sarah finish taping the last two streamers onto the dining table's overhead lamp. When complete, Sarah steps back, looks the room over and remarks, "Excellent! Everything is perfect!" Carl takes a seat and glances at his watch, "Tommy's just getting off work. He should be here in about ten minutes!" Everybody buzzes with excitement as the time gets close for the Birthday Boy's arrival. BIG ENGINE RUMBLE. TIRES ON CRUSHED GRAVEL. Sarah peeks out the front living room window. She pivots about with glee, "He's here! Okay everybody - stay quiet - this is a Surprise!" All the people get quiet and everyone hears the car door slam and footsteps approach the house - as Tommy pushes open the front door and comes inside - Everyone Yells "SURPRISE!" Tommy stops momentarily frozen in the open doorway as he sees the room full of smiles and friendly faces. Sarah rushes up and gives Tommy a kiss and remarks, "Hope you like your surprise honey?" Tommy hugs Sarah and shakes his head with a big grin, "Didn't have a clue Sweetie! (Looks about) Sure is great to see everyone!" Sarah leaves for the kitchen as Tommy shuts the door and proceeds to go through the room shaking hands and greeting his friends. Carl joins Sarah in the kitchen to help bring out the plates, cutlery, and glasses. Sarah's mom and two lady friends have been busy in the kitchen arranging various trays of tasty appetizers and scrumptious food - Southern Fried Chicken, BBQ Ribs, Pizza, Home Fries, delicious meatloaf, buttered corn cobs, potato salad, coleslaw, and jello rings. And later on for desert, there's apple pie and pumpkin pie with Parlour Ice Cream, and the "pièce de résistance" - a scrumptious three-layer chocolate Birthday Cake. Sarah, Carl, and the ladies carry out the trays of food to cover the dining table. Sarah cheerfully announces, "The food's ready! Okay everyone - Time to eat!" All the people get up to grab plates, utensils, glasses, and start to load up on the yummy eatables spread out before them. Soon, everybody is seated with a heaping plate of food and begin to enjoy the delicious feast. The living room gets filled with conversation, laughter, and happy faces. Tommy and Sarah sit on the sofa with two friends and reminisce of former High School days. All around them, everyone is having a wonderful time, everyone enjoying the special celebration!

While Tommy is busy with a couple buddies that made their way over to chat, Sarah stands up and glances over to Carl and winks her eye. Carl smiles, nods, then gets up and goes to the kitchen with Sarah. In the kitchen, Sarah holds the birthday cake as Carl lights the candles. With candles burning bright, Sarah, Carl, and the three moms, walk into the living room - Sarah starts the familiar tune known around the world - "Happy Birthday to you - Happy Birthday to you." Everyone in the room merrily joins in to sing along as Sarah walks over and lowers the cake onto Tommy's lap. The young man has an expression of both delight and tiny embarrassment…delight at the stunning three-layer cake and glowing candles…and slightly embarrassed, as everyone crowds around him singing, making him the centre of attention. The years of Ninjan training has changed Tommy's nature to be humble, quiet and reserved - no longer the brash teenager as before. Today, he's a young man of depth, discipline, and deference.

A friend yells, "Blow out the candles, Tommy and make a wish!" All the family and friends playfully edge him on. Tommy looks at Sarah, gives a big smile, takes a deep breath and blows across the candles to extinguish all the burning flames. As little trails of white smoke rise off the candle wicks, Sarah reaches down to retrieve the cake and carry it over to the dining table, where she divides the cake into serving portions. The people return to their chairs, and friendly conversation fills the room again. Sarah cuts a 'hero portion' and brings the first piece of cake over to Tommy with a sweet smile, a little kiss, and whispers, "Here, hon,…chocolate cake is your favourite!" Tommy holds the plate, kisses Sarah on the cheek, and replies, "Sweetheart, after everyone's gone - let's have a special time - just the two of us!" Sarah smiles, "I'd like that honey! Just you and me." Sarah leaves to go into the kitchen to help the ladies.

Later that evening after everyone has gone home, the kitchen clean and tidy with the dishes, glasses and cutlery washed and put away; Sarah and Tommy sit cosy on the sofa while soft music plays in the background. The two sweethearts still have that 'Spark' that began their love five years ago, when they caught each other's eye as students at the Dojo. Sarah leans in and snuggles close, Tommy drapes his arm over her shoulder and pulls her tight against his side. He gazes down at the pretty young lady resting so peacefully next to him. Tommy smiles warmly as he tenderly brushes Sarah's hair, gently caressing the soft skin of her face. Tommy leans his head and softly kisses the top of Sarah's head, "Sweetheart, Thank You for making my Birthday so special!" Sarah lifts her eyes and smiles wide, "Honey, I'm so glad you liked it!" Tommy gives her a kiss and remarks, "Liked it - I loved it! That Katana sword decoration on the cake was amazing! Your mom did a super job." Sarah nods, "Mom's always been a great cook (pause) I hope to cook as good as her when we have our own home." Tommy gives a reassuring squeeze and grins, "Babe, you're a fantastic cook already (pats his tummy) I should know." They both laugh! Sarah and Tommy rest peacefully as romantic music fills the room with songs of tender love.

# CHAPTER THREE
*Tommy and Sarah Talk*

Tommy revs the supped-up engine of his blue Ford Mustang as the car zooms down the highway. It's almost time to for Sarah to get off work at the Regional Hospital - Tommy doesn't want to be late picking up his sweetheart. He watches the tachometer as he pops the clutch and shifts into 4<sup>th</sup> gear - the shift makes the mustang lunge forward from the extra horsepower. The car tears down the asphalt road toward the medical facility just a few miles away. Tommy glances at his wristwatch - 4:55 pm. If all goes well, he should be able to be on time for Sarah to have her ride home after a gruelling day at the Hospital. The Nurse Supervisor had asked Sarah to work some additional hours because a fellow nurse was unable to show up, and Sarah kindly obliged. Now, that she's no longer on nursing duty, Tommy knows his girlfriend is bone-tired, hungry, and ready to go home to eat, and get a much deserved rest. Tommy rounds the bend in the highway and spots the Hospital building on the horizon. He presses the gas pedal - VROOM!

Sarah exits the sliding glass-aluminum doors of the Hospital entrance and walks out onto the front cement steps. She looks around the nearby parking lot for the blue Mustang, but doesn't see it. As Tommy approaches the Hospital grounds, he sees Sarah standing on the entrance steps - he taps the car horn to send out a few friendly BEEPS! Sarah recognizes Tommy's car horn and turns toward the direction of the sound. She smiles to see her handsome fella drive into the parking lot and steer the car to the bottom of the front steps. Tommy rolls down his car window and remarks, "Glad I made it in time! Wouldn't want to miss picking up my Sweetheart!" Sarah descends the steps with renewed energy and big smile, "There's my man! Missed you Honey

Bun!" Sarah reaches Tommy's open window, leans in and gives him a quick peck on the lips. Tommy grins, "I've been missing you too!" He pauses speaking as Sarah swings around the car to get into the front passenger seat, shuts the door and looks at her beau. Tommy smiles and continues, "When we get to your folks place and have supper, we need to talk about something important!" Sarah sweeps back some fallen stands of her long hair and comments, "Is this about going to College? You know I think you'd be great in Construction!" Tommy moves the gear shift and Sarah buckles up. As Tommy eases the car out of the Hospital parking lot and motors back onto the highway, he remarks, "No Sweetie, It's not about College?" Sarah looks at Tommy with a big smile and chimes in, "Then you're gonna stay at the Garage, right?" Tommy glances at his girl and sees her happy expectation. He replies in a quiet manner, "No Hon, I'm not taking the offer to stay on as an Auto Mechanic!" Sarah's joyful countenance changes to that of unexpected surprise, "Then, if it's not College or staying at the Garage - what is it?" Tommy drives with his eyes on the road ahead, turns his gaze at Sarah and replies, "I'll explain it all after we eat at your folks place, then go for our evening walk." Sarah studies Tommy as he's driving. She turns her eyes and stares as the ribbon of asphalt approaches, only to disappear under the car. She reaches out to touch Tommy's hand on the gearshift. Tommy glances at Sarah and gives a loving reassuring smile, "After supper, you'll know everything - talking about it while driving the car is not the place or time for it." Sarah nods and leans in to give a sweet little kiss on Tommy cheek. Both sweethearts smile as the Mustang travels the highway toward Sarah's parent's farm, the place where as a little girl - Sarah grew up with lots of animals and wide open spaces.

# CHAPTER FOUR
## *The Canopy of Stars*

The evening air is warm and relaxing as Tommy and Carl sit on lawn chairs under the canopy of stars that fill the night sky. The "Hoot" of an owl from the trees catches their attention. Carl raises his tumbler of cool lemonade and remarks, "It's likely ready to pounce on some unsuspecting field mouse." Tommy grins and comments, "Amazing how creatures can see in the dark!" The grandfather shifts his frame in the lawn chair and leans toward Tommy, "All of God's creatures have amazing abilities. The daytime ones and the nighttime ones. (Pause) And people have special abilities too - like you, Tommy!" The young man looks at Carl, "What do you mean grandpa?" The elderly man gazes at his grandson for a few seconds, then replies, "You've always had a way with mechanical things - tinkering with cars and stuff. You're smart, strong, and athletic, not to mention quick and spry. Then, there's your excellent Ninjan skills. I should know - I trained you!" Tommy smiles his appreciation, "I owe all that to you, Grandpa! Your teaching and patience over the years made me a Ninjan Master." Tommy nods slightly with a respectful bow, "You will always be my Sensi!" Carl smiles deeply at hearing such words. He leans back, tilts his head to look at the array of glowing stars overhead. Carl comments, "Where ever you go, Tommy, look up at the stars and remember - no matter how things change all around you, the stars stay the same. That's comforting! In the old days, the stars pointed people home." Tommy gazes up at the stars and remains quiet for a number of seconds, then remarks, "Grandpa, I've made my decision - Sarah and I talked it over, and I'm not staying at the garage or going to College, (pause) I'm joining the US Army!" Carl turns to his grandson with a big smile, "Tommy, I'm proud of you! You'll make a fine soldier." Tommy extends his tumbler to imply a Toast, "Well, Grandpa! Here's to the exciting road ahead!" Carl lifts his arm and clinks his tumbler to Tommy's glass, "Here's to you! A fine grandson, and soon - a fine soldier!" Both grin as they drink back their lemonade.

# CHAPTER FIVE

## *Tommy Joins The United States Army*

The Auto Shop is bustling more than usual. Barry, Tommy and others, are working on cars, trucks and vans up on hoists. The puttering sound of the air compressor provides a steady background noise. The air guns, clanging metal, and engine motors, fill the Garage with the traditional sounds of mechanics fixing vehicles. Tommy is bent over an engine ratcheting down a part when Barry passes by carrying a new muffler pipe. Tommy lifts up and calls out, "Barry. Barry." His boss stops and steps over nearby, "What is it Tommy?" The young man takes a shallow breath and replies, "There's something I need to talk with you about." Barry smiles and remarks, "Okay! After you finish tightening those bolts on Mrs. Cameron's car, we'll talk in the office." Tommy nods and Barry heads to the other side of the Shop with the muffler part.

Later on, Tommy sits in Barry's office as his boss settles into his well-worn brown leather office chair. Barry gives Tommy a curious look, smiles and asks, "So Tommy, what's up?" Tommy clears his throat and replies, "Barry, you're a great boss, and I really like working at the Garage." Barry smiles and remarks, "You're finally going to take my offer and become one of my permanent Crew!" Tommy looks at Barry with a respectful expression and replies, "I really appreciate your offer - You're an excellent boss and this is a great place to work (Pause) But, I've decided to leave and wanted to let you know." Barry is stunned a bit and leans back in his chair to digest what's been said. The older man remarks, "I guess I got use to the idea of having you around - you're a good mechanic!" Tommy leans in to comment, "I talked it over a lot with Grandpa - and I've decided to join the Army!" Barry stares at the young man for a bit, then breaks into a big grin, stands up and extends his arm to shake Tommy's hand, "Congratulations Tommy! I'm proud of you, and proud of your choice!" Tommy shakes his boss's hand with relief, "Thanks Barry! I wanted you to know as soon as possible." Barry puts his hand on Tommy's shoulder, "Just remember, you've always got a place here at the Shop." Tommy smiles and remarks, "That's good to know. I appreciate that - Well, better get back to work - Mrs. Cameron's car won't fix itself." Barry waves his hand and teases, "Get back to work, kid - you're on the clock!" Tommy nods, "You got it boss!" The man watches Tommy leave his office. Barry turns his gaze to the wall shelf with a framed photo of Barry, Carl and friends. Barry picks up the photo, his eyes focus on Carl and he whispers, "You did well, old friend, - he's a great kid!"

# CHAPTER SIX
## *The Recruiting Office*

Tommy scans around at the city buildings as Carl steers the car into a parking spot by the curb. The downtown traffic is busy with folks going to work, running errands, or shopping the retail stores. Carl cuts the engine and glances at Tommy, "Finally here - let's get out!" The duo exit the car and stand on the sidewalk outside the street-level Army Recruiting Office. Tommy's eyes fix on the Poster of a young man and woman dressed in Military uniform in the storefront window. Carl puts his hand on Tommy's shoulder and comments with a smile, "So proud of you, Tommy!" The grandson smiles and remarks, "I'm glad you're here, Grandpa. You'll be the last familiar face I see before enlisting - after that, everyone is gonna be a stranger!" Carl replies, "You'll meet some great people, Tommy - fellow soldiers and friends for life!" The young man eyes the entry door, looks at his grandpa and grins, "Time to sign up for my country!" Carl puts his hand across Tommy's shoulder and gives an encouraging, "HOORAH!"

Tommy pushes the glass door open and the two step inside and approach a middle-aged man wearing a clean crisp Army uniform with Sergeant stripes. The Officer lifts his gaze off his paperwork and smiles a greeting, "Good Day! I'm Sergeant Davis. Welcome to the Army Recruitment Office. How can I help you?" Tommy takes a step forward, makes eye contact and announces, "I'm here to enlist, Sir!" The Sergeant glances at the grandfather with a smile and remarks, "That's wonderful son! The Army is always ready for strong young recruits like you." The Officer stretches his arm to the right and retrieves a clipboard with an Enlistment Form which he places on the counter in front of Tommy. The Officer places a pen on the clipboard and instructs, "Step One. Please fill out the Application Form and hand it in." Tommy pursues the paperwork and gives a quick glance at Carl. The experienced Recruiter anticipates what Tommy is thinking and comments, "Step Two. Army Staff will give you a Medical Exam. Step Three. You read and sign the Enlistment Contract." Tommy looks at the Sergeant and nods. The young man turns toward the row of chairs lined up against the wall and strides over and sits down. Carl follows to take a seat beside him. Tommy grips the pen and proceeds through the Application Form filling in the blanks with his information. He double checks the Form, puts his name at the bottom of the Application, stands up and brings it back to the Officer. The Officer scans the Application and smiles, "Everything's in order. Please wait here and someone will take you to our Medical Officer." Tommy pivots about and goes to sit down next to Carl. Tommy sits stoic and silent, except for his bouncing knee that betrays his nervous energy. Carl pats his grandson's hand and remarks, "A routine Medical exam - just like you've had before!" Tommy nods and grins. As they watch pedestrians walk by through the Recruitment Office windows, a young woman in her twenties with hair pinned back in a neat Army uniform approaches, "Tommy, if you will please follow me, the Medical Officer will see you now." Tommy stands up and follows the young lady past the counter and down a hallway with various doors - one is open. The young lady stops and gestures to the room's interior, then turns and walks away. Tommy stands at the doorway, and looks to see a man at a desk next to an examination table. The Army Major lifts his eyes toward Tommy and remarks, "Hi Tommy! Please come in, shut the door and sit on the Examination table." Tommy enters the room, closes the door and gets a spot on top the table's padded vinyl surface. The Officer steps near with clipboard and pen in hand, "All recruits need to clear a basic Medical as part of their Application. When recruits arrive at the Military Base, they get a thorough Physical Exam. Tommy, please open your shirt." Tommy unbuttons his shirt and waits as Major Mikels places his Stethoscope on Tommy's chest and comments, "Now, take a deep breath and hold till I say release."

In the Recruitment Office waiting room, Carl pulls out his cell phone to see the time - it's only been 15 minutes since Tommy left. He pockets his phone and reaches for a magazine when he hears Tommy's approach. Carl asks, "How did it go?" The grandson replies with a shrug, "Okay I guess - got a quick Medical to see if I'm fit enough to enlist." Carl tilts his head with a mild chuckle, "It appears you passed!" Tommy sits beside Carl and glances at the magazine and exclaims, "Golf. When do you ever golf?" The grandfather grins, "It's a great sport. Lots of people golf. (Chuckle) But on the Reservation it'd be the reverse, we'd probably call 'Flog'! That's because we have tons of sand and so little grass. It'd be one giant sand trap!" Tommy laughs, "Flog. Good one Grandpa!" As they both share a humorous moment. The Recruiting Sergeant comes over to them, "Tommy. You passed the Enlistment Medical - Now, we need you to read and sign the Commitment Form and take the Oath." Tommy comments in surprise, "Oath?" The Sergeant replies in a polite professional manner, "Every Recruit for the US Military is required to take an Oath to serve these United Sates as part of their official Enlistment." The young man looks at his grandfather and stands to his feet before the Sergeant, and gives a firm nod. The Sergeant points down the hall to where another Officer stands next to a doorway. Tommy and the Recruiter walk to the Officer at the doorway, and all three enter the room and close the door. Carl watches with expectation. A quarter hour passes before the door opens and Sergeant Davis and Tommy emerge and come down the hallway toward the seating area. Carl fixes his eyes on Tommy, the lad walks with determination, his shoulders back and head held high, his smile has the expression of accomplishment and satisfaction. When they reach the chairs, Tommy sits down next to Carl while the Officer leaves and resumes his position behind the counter. Carl notices his grandson's eyes - there's been a change, things seem different. Tommy turns to his grandfather wide-eyed and remarks, "Grandpa, something happened in that room when I signed the Commitment Form and spoke the Oath! - Something I never felt before. (Pause) After I spoke those words, I felt this strong connection to my country  - like there's an invisible cord connecting me to America, and America to me!" Carl looks at Tommy with deep love and respect, "That's what it is like when a couple say their marriage vows, or when parents see their newborn baby - a powerful connection takes place!" Tommy listens to his grandpa's words. Carl continues, "The moment you spoke the Oath to Serve your country, that connection took place - that's because you spoke the Oath from your heart!" Tommy sits back in the chair with a keen realization of what he just went through. At that moment, Sergeant Davis walks over and announces, "Congratulations Tommy! Your Application, Medical, and Enlistment Form are processed - You are now a member of the United States Army." The Officer hands Tommy an envelope with documentation inside and remarks, "Be here this coming Tuesday at 0900 hours. A Bus will be here to pick up the new recruits." The Sergeant looks squarely at Tommy and salutes, "Soldier. Welcome to the United States Army!" Tommy snaps to attention, raises his arm in a salute and replies firmly, "Thank You, Sir!" Sergeant Davis smiles, pivots about and returns to his position at the counter. Carl puts his hand on Tommy's shoulder and exclaims, "Tuesday. That only gives you 5 more days as a civilian!" Tommy grins and replies, "5 days. Grandpa! I'm ready to go now!" The older man smiles at his grandson's youthful enthusiasm. With near watery eyes, Carl remarks, "Well you may be ready, but I'm not - I'd like some more days with you - after that, the Army has you and I won't be able to see you as before." Tommy smiles and puts his arm around his grandpa's shoulder and comments, "Let's go home and celebrate! I'd like to eat a nice steak!" Carl grins. The grandfather and grandson exit the Recruitment Office glass doors and step out onto the city street. As Carl and Tommy stand on the sidewalk, Tommy looks up at the United States Flag flapping in the breeze over the Recruitment Office entrance. His eyes trace over the 'Stars and Stripes', Tommy notices the flag's colours - the vibrant red, the sparkling white, and the deep blue. At that moment, it's like he's seeing the American Flag for the very first time - there's a small lump in his throat as he considers all that the US Flag stands for - more than ever before, Tommy feels a new sense of pride and loyalty. Tommy takes a deep breath and stands tall. He turns to his grandpa and remarks, "I'm ready to Serve! - God! Country! Family!" Carl gazes tenderly at his grandson, puts his hand on Tommy's shoulder and replies, "I'm so proud of you, Tommy! Plum proud of your decision to join the Army! (Smiles) Now, let's go celebrate with a nice steak!" Tommy grins and pipes out, "HOORAH!"

# CHAPTER SEVEN
## *Saying Good Bye*

Tommy and Sarah snuggle under a blanket, as they sit on a log in front of a roaring campfire. The lively flames send sparks and tiny red embers upward only to disappear in the night sky above. The warmth and sight of a crackling campfire brings a soothing comfort to the soul. Whether it's watching the wood burn, only to fall and change position, or the dancing flames and glowing embers, people are somehow drawn to the fire - watching, studying, staring at the flames - as if mesmerized by something ancient and timeless - like when man discovered fire. In our collective experience, when we sit in front of a burning campfire or fireplace to gaze at the moving flames, there are moments - moments when we ourselves seem to be discovering fire for the very first time!

Sarah takes a lingering look at Tommy, his face illuminated by the fire. She leans in, drapes her arm over his shoulder, and firmly plants a kiss on his lips. Tommy responds as young men do when kissed by their sweethearts - he kisses her back with intensity and passion. As the two lovers break for air, Tommy asks, "What was that all about?" Sarah brushes her bangs aside and gives a sweet smile, "This is our last night before you leave!" She giggles and gives a playful shove, "You can keep staring at that fire - but just so you know - I'm hotter!" Tommy grins and grabs Sarah's two arms and draws her close, "You were hot the first time I saw you - at the Dojo five years ago!" Sarah leans her head against Tommy's chest and whispers, "I thought you were very handsome back then!" Tommy teases, "Hey! Handsome back then! What about now?" Sarah squirms to break free but Tommy is too strong. She laughs, "Don't worry - I still think you're handsome!" Tommy bends his head down with 'puppy-dog-eyes', "You know you're the only girl for me. Only you!" Sarah caves at Tommy's tender words and hugs him tight, "Tommy, I'm gonna miss you so much! Four years seems such a long time." Tommy gazes at his girl with affection, "We'll just have to stay in touch a lot. Every day when possible." Sarah smiles and repeats, "Every day when possible!" Tommy and Sarah share a lingering romantic kiss under the cover of twinkling stars overhead. The burning logs of the campfire shift, sending out bright red embers that float upward to drift and disappear in the dark night sky.

# CHAPTER EIGHT

*A Bus of Recruits*

Lots of people have gathered on the city sidewalk. Families, parents, siblings, sweethearts, friends; all wanting to say 'bye' to their son, brother, boyfriend, schoolmate, that's headed for the Army. There are plenty of hugs, kisses, photos, pats on the back, and that reassuring hand on the shoulder. Tommy, Sarah and Carl, took a spot close to the Recruiting Office grey brick exterior, and simply watch and observe. The lively crowd leave little room for pedestrians to go by, some shoppers briefly step onto the road surface to walk past the scattered clusters. Tommy scans about to observe how his fellow recruits are. Some appear somewhat nervous or uneasy, perhaps uncomfortable or embarrassed at their mothers fawning over their 'baby' leaving home. Other guys seem cool and collect, fortified by an inner resolve about joining the Army. Carl glances over at Tommy and Sarah, reaches into his pant pocket to bring out a smooth thick round metal disk - and extends it. Tommy opens his hand and Carl places the silver medallion in his grandson's palm. Tommy looks at the medallion, quickly glances at Sarah, then turns to Carl to remark, "What's this Grandpa?" By now, Sarah is intrigued and slides her fingertips over the engraved characters on the medallion surface. Carl smiles and replies, "That is a rare Japanese Token - a little gift to you!" Tommy eyes the engraving and asks, "What does it mean?" Carl steps closer to make sure he's heard over the chatter of the surrounding crowd, "The Japanese Kanji engraving means Warrior - over time it came to represent Bravery and Honour! I want you to carry it with you at all times." Tommy clasps his fingers over the Token and gives a humble bow, "Sensi, Grandfather, I will keep it with me as you have asked!" Tommy slips the silver medallion into his front jean pocket.

* * *

At that moment, a large bus painted in Army green with tinted windows, rolls up in front of the Recruitment Office, parks, and opens the front access door. From the back of the crowd booms a strong voice in military style, "Recruits, say your goodbye and get ready to board the bus!" The Recruitment Office Sergeant is wearing sunglasses and stands with a clipboard and whistle. Teary-eyed mothers take a final hug, fathers shake their son's hand, and girlfriends give lingering kisses. The Sergeant strides to the bus and positions at the side of the bus door, clipboard in hand, he scans the papers and begins calling out names. Upon hearing their name, each recruit grabs his gear and climbs aboard the bus. The Sergeant bellows, "Long Grass. Tommy Long Grass!" Sarah grabs Tommy to give a quick kiss. Carl extends his arm to shake Tommy's hand, "You'll be in our thoughts and prayers!" Tommy responds, "Thanks Grandpa!" The young man smiles at Sarah and Carl, clutches his duffle bag, walks to the bus, ascends the steps, and disappears into the bus interior.

Tommy spots an empty seat on the right, halfway down the aisle, he sits down and stores the duffle bag by his side. He watches Carl and Sarah still standing on the sidewalk, but they can't see Tommy because of the opaque windows. As the last recruit gets on the bus and is seated, the soldier driving the bus starts the engine and shifts into gear. The people wave to the bus as it drives off into the traffic lane. Tommy strains his neck to get a lingering glimpse of Sarah and Carl, as the bus gets further down the road. Tommy turns about and gets comfortable. He peers around the bus at the other lads. Most are close to his age, except some that seem a few years older. He notices the guys' heads of hair - a varied assortment  - trendy Salon-styled, neat trimmed hipsters, wild loose skaters, shorthair varsity cuts, and a couple skinheads. Tommy sits back mindful of his long raven black hair just past his shoulders. The Military bus motors through city streets and reaches the highway. Different guys are talking back and forth like old teammates, others are quiet and reflective - wondering what awaits them at the Army Base. Some have heard the 'horror stories' of Boot Camp, no doubt circulated to strike fear in a recruit's heart. From the sombre faces on a couple lads, the question lingers, "Are the stories true? What's it really like?" The driver shifts gear to put the bus into highway speed. Tommy looks out his window at the countryside. He soaks in the opportunity to see family farms, ranches, and residential hamlets go by. He knows from conversations with Grandpa Carl, once you arrive at Boot Camp, you're no longer 'free-to-do' as you please; you, and all that you are - emotionally, mentally, physically, and all your time - now, belong to the Army! Tommy leans his head back to grab some shut-eye, he listens to the steady drone of bus tires rolling on the highway.

# CHAPTER NINE
*Flying High*

The Military bus exits the highway and drives directly to the Airfield ringed by chain-link fence. The signage declares the airfield belongs to the United States Air Force. Tommy and the other recruits peer out the windows to see big cargo planes, F-16 Fighter jets, and Black Hawk helicopters. The bus driver steers the vehicle onto the wide flat tarmac, toward an olive grey Transport plane with a deployed cargo ramp at the back. A group of Military personnel stand nearby.

The bus full of the twenty recruits approaches fifty yards from the plane and stops. The driver cuts the engine and opens the bus door. An Officer leaves the group standing by the plane, walks to the bus and ascends the steps to stand at the front. The Officer announces, "Recruits. Disembark the bus and gather together beside the aircraft ramp." The Officer steps off the bus, stands to the side as he watches the recruits exit the bus one by one. Tommy grabs his duffle bag, lines up behind a fellow recruit and moves to the front door. He descends the bus steps onto the tarmac, and makes his way to where the guys have gathered. The Officer beside the bus, goes inside to check the bus is empty of recruits, then he exits and rejoins the Military personnel.

The assembled young men stand in a loose civilian manner, their bags and gear by their side. The lads watch as the Military Officers stride toward them and stop ten feet away. An Officer, an Army Major, steps forward and looks the faces of the recruits, "This plane will fly you across America to an army Base in Georgia, where you will begin your Training." The Officer scans the recruits, then another Officer steps up beside him and remarks, "Now Recruits, grab your gear, walk up the ramp and take a seat on the plane." He glances about the recruits as they stand motionless as if 'put-on-pause'. The Officer yells, "Move out now! Move! Move! Move!" The recruits bolt into action, grab their gear and make haste up the plane's cargo ramp, going into the plane. Once inside, the recruits can see how big and cavernous the cargo interior is. Military planes can transport - Tanks, Armoured Personnel Vehicles, weapons and armaments, and loads of equipment and supplies. A Corporal at his station inside the cargo bay, directs the recruits to sit in the seats along the side interior. Each seat is fitted with a safety harness. The Corporal watches as the young men get seated and buckle into their harness. Tommy observes his fellow recruits - some have an expression of dread indicating they uncomfortable flying. With all the recruits seated and strapped in, the Corporal resumes his position and stands "At Ease". The Army Major and the other personnel ascend the cargo ramp. The Corporal stands at Attention and salutes the Major, "The recruits are seated and secure." The Major salutes the Corporal, glances at the row of recruits and comments, "Tell the Pilot we are ready! Close the cargo door." The Corporal salutes, "Yes Sir!", then he pivots about and goes toward the front to the plane. Within a minute, there's the sound of powerful motors lifting the big metal ramp of the transport plane, locking it secure into flight position. A loud whirling sound fills the interior as the plane's large jet engines start up. The Transport plane begins to taxi to the runway. Inside the aircraft, Tommy and the recruits can feel the bumps and jars as the plane gains speed and velocity going down the runway. Soon, the entire plane vibrates as it reaches greater speed - then Takes Off! Everything's quiet as the plane ascends the sky at a steep angle, then levels off high above the clouds, heading toward the East coast.

# CHAPTER TEN
*Army Boot Camp*

The big Military cargo plane lands at an airstrip on the American East Coast. Tommy and the other recruits transfer to another Military bus that drives them to the Military Base. The bus pulls up and stops at the Main Gate Check Point. The Recruits watch as serious-looking guards with automatic weapons check the bus driver's paperwork, nods approval, then waves to move forward. The driver shifts gear and drives through the Main Gate, past the perimeter chain link fence, and onto the grounds of the sprawling Army Base. Numerous buildings, roadways, structures, and exercise fields, cover the vast military complex. Tommy looks out his window to see groups of soldiers busy - marching, exercising, drilling, and training. The driver manoeuvres the bus through a couple roadways, until approaching a two-story cement building up ahead. The driver comes to a stop, shifts into park and cuts the engine. Two Officers in crisp clean military uniform approach the bus, one is a Lieutenant, the other a Drill Sergeant. The Lieutenant climbs up the bus, stands at the front, and calls out in a loud clear voice, "Recruits! Disembark the bus and fall in!" The Officer promptly turns, quickly descends, and positions beside the Sergeant. The two Officers keenly watch as the new recruits climb off the bus and stand in a loose group. The faces of the young men reflect high school, freshman college, and youthful inexperience. All the lads fix their gaze on the two men standing before them.

The Lieutenant takes a step forward, "My name is Lieutenant Philips! Welcome to Reception Battalion! Over the next number of days, you will get an Army Haircut, a complete Physical Exam including Blood and Urine tests, Inoculations, and distribution of your Army gear - uniforms, duffle bag, and mouth guard. After you have received those things - you are going to get basic instruction on standing, marching, and upkeep of Barracks." The Officer glances across the faces of the young men, and continues, "Forget what you heard about the Army! Forget what you thought about the Army! Put it all away. - As of this moment, you are Property of the United States of America! You're no longer the High School Quarter Back, the cool kid with the fast car, or the 'Big Man' on Campus - As of now, and for the next four years - you are - and will become - United States Army Soldiers!" The officer watches as some lads shift about, and others fidget. The Lieutenant extends his arm to the man on his right, "This is Sergeant O'Toole - Your Drill Sergeant!" The Sergeant steps forward, stands with authority as he scans the group, "Everyone Fall In - form two straight rows of 10!" The Officers watch as the young men spring into action, jostling about to quickly form two uneven rows that zig-zag back and forth. The Sergeant bellows, "Attention! Eyes front. Stand straight and tall - No moving about!" The men observe the lads stiffen their posture, stand straight and stare ahead. Sergeant O'Toole strides along the first row, then walks in front of the second row. He studies the face and form of each recruit. He positions himself at the front of the two rows and yells, "Okay recruits! Everyone, except the last man on my right, extend your left arm shoulder level." The Sergeant looks as the recruits position arms - making the gaps even more noticeable. The Drill Sergeant orders, "Standing straight, eyes ahead, shift sideways until your fingertips touch the other recruit's shoulder." There's the sound of boots and shoes shuffling across the pavement until the two rows appear straight and even. The Sergeant smiles approval and remarks, "Put your arm down! (He scans the group of newbies) That's your first drill lesson - forming a straight line!" He returns to stand next to his fellow soldier, and gives the Lieutenant a nod. The Lieutenant looks at the young men lined up in military fashion and comments, "Sergeant O'Toole will take you to Stage 1 of Reception Battalion - Your Haircut! The Lieutenant looks at Tommy and a couple lads with shoulder length hair) Dismissed!" The lieutenant turns and walks away. Sergeant O'Toole grins and remarks, "Okay, grab your gear and follow me." Tommy and the rest of the guys latch onto their stuff and follow their Drill Sergeant over the wide Parade Grounds toward the array of buildings on the far side. The Sergeant leads the group through a set of open double doors, down a wide corridor and through a doorway on the left. The recruits enter a large wide room where chairs are lined up in a row, where a soldier holding an electric razor stands beside each chair. Sergeant O'Toole remarks, "Time for your Army Buzz Cut!" The lads set down their belongings and the first set of guys take a chair as the others watch. The minute each recruit sits down, the soldier places one hand to steady the recruit's head, and with the other hand runs the buzzing hair clipper to shave the scalp from front to back. Piles of hair fall off each recruit's head leaving the lad's head near bald. As soon as one recruit gets buzzed and stands up, the soldier waves another recruit to fill the chair. Sergeant O'Toole observes as the batch of his new recruits look identical in their fresh Army Buzz Cut. Some of the lads run their finger tips over the bare scalp with facial expressions of shock and mild horror. Everyone has a bald head. Everyone feeling totally different!

With his troop sporting new haircuts, the Sergeant waves his group to follow and leads them out of the room, down the hall and into a large room with a number of chairs, examination tables, curtained stalls, and Military nurses and personnel. Sergeant O'Toole comments, "This is where you get the Army Physical Exam and your Inoculations." As he finishes speaking, various Army personnel approach with clipboards and call out recruit names. Each recruit goes to the Examination table and undergoes a complete Medical Exam. At the Tables, the nurses takes blood samples, and hand the recruits a clear plastic canister for the urine sample, then point to the curtained stalls. When each recruit returns the urine sample, the nurse gives a set of Inoculations. The entire process is quick and methodical, and soon, all the recruits have been Examined and Inoculated. Each lad takes a chair and remains seated, awaiting further instructions.

Sergeant O'Toole looks at the guys and comments, "Let's get your Army gear!" The group get up and follow the Drill Sergeant out of the large room, up the hall, across the pavement to enter a large hanger type building with rows of tables stacked with Military uniforms, boots, helmet, and gear. At these stations, soldiers behind the tables distribute the proper size uniforms to each recruit. Tommy is muscular and fit and receives an X-Large uniform to accommodate his physique. The young men are given duffle bags, and Army-Issue backpacks that contain boots, helmet, tactical knife, field canteen, belt, socks, 2 white t-shirts, and Army cap with visor. Sergeant O'Toole looks on as the recruits become loaded down with even more stuff than they brought - every lad not only holds his own belonging from home - now, each one has to carry their Army duffle bag, and their backpack filled with Army-Issue gear.

A few of the lads can hardly manage to stand let alone walk. Sergeant O'Toole waves the group forward and leads them across the wide Parade Grounds and over the grassy field toward rows of Barracks. Each Barrack has a large NUMBER above the entrance. The Sergeant with recruits in tow walk among the Barracks until the man stops. Sergeant O'Toole lifts his hand and points to the structure, "Barrack 30 is your new home! Let's Go inside." The group enter and the young men notice the clean interior with crisp tidy bunks. Sergeant O'Toole quips, "Okay soldiers, get a bunk, store your gear, and put on the uniform you just received." The guys quickly disburse to head toward their selected bunk. Tommy grabs a bunk halfway on the right side of the open interior. All the guys have got a bunk, and now, everyone begins to put away their belongings and switch into their army uniform. Tommy opens his duffle bag and loads his stuff into the side Cabinet, and foot locker at the end of his bed. As the recruits are busy, the Sergeant looks at his wrist watch, "It's 1300 hours now. Mess Hall is at 1500 hours. For those unaware of military time - you got 2 hours before supper. Get squared away, freshen up, and be in uniform. I'll meet you at 1445 sharp!" The recruits nod and Sergeant O'Toole and exits the Barracks. Tommy and his fellow recruits get busy arranging their bunk area, filling foot lockers, storing clothes, and packing away gear. The minutes pass quickly. As Tommy lifts his eyes to check his wristwatch - 1443 hours. One of the guys yells out, "It's almost time!" The company of new recruits move quick to get ready, some guys checking that others' uniforms are in order.

Just like clockwork - Sergeant O'Toole enters the barracks at exactly 1445 sharp. The man scans the interior, his eyes darting here and there across the bunks, lockers and wardrobe units. Everything neat, tidy and shipshape, just the way he likes it. The Sergeant smiles and announces in an authoritative voice, "Line up by twos - we're going to the Mess Hall like a company of soldiers!" The guys quickly manoeuvre and jostle about to form two parallel lines, standing at Attention awaiting further instructions. Sergeant O'Toole grins and remarks, "Okay soldiers, are you ready for some chow?" The company reply in a loud voice. "Yes Sir!" Sergeant O'Toole can't resist the moment, steps out to better view the recruits, and bellows, "I can't hear you - are you  ready to eat?" The entire company of young lads YELL out, "YES SIR!!" Sergeant O'Toole grins again, points to the entrance and pipes up. "Well, what are you waiting for? Get going!" At those orders, the Sergeant leads his company out the front door. The entire company empty out of the barracks and follow Sergeant O'Toole on the pathway toward a large building that's the Army Base Mess Hall. Entering the building, the Sergeant and company briefly stand in an open area. Sergeant O'Toole points to the Mess Hall counter with bins of trays, plates, cups, and cutlery, "Grab a tray, get your utensils and beverage cup - then proceed along the counter to get your meal." Tommy and his fellow soldiers grab their stuff, line up, and go along the counter where Mess Hall Staff give each lad a plate of meatloaf with gravy, mash potatoes, vegetables, and a piece of pie for dessert - either apple, cherry or pumpkin. The Sergeant is the last to get his food. He looks at his company, all the young men hold their meal trays and await his direction. The man sees the hungry expressions in their eyes and remarks, "We pick a unit table, sit and chow down!" He leads the group over to a section with empty tables and motions to sit. The lads rapidly get seated and begin to dig into the comfort food of tasty meatloaf and mash potatoes covered by delicious gravy. Tommy eyes his plate and smiles wide - meatloaf is one of his favourites. As his recruits are busy eating their meal, Sergeant O'Toole scans the faces of his company - trying to memorize each recruits look and physical features. Over the years of being a Drill Sergeant, the man has learned the sooner you identify your company soldiers, the better for Basic Training - after all - a Drill Sergeant has to know who he is YELLING at! The man looks across the tables and smiles - his new recruits are chowing down their first taste of Army food.

After his troop has finished eating, Sergeant O'Toole instructs them to return the plastic meal trays to the counter. Then the Sergeant and recruits exit the Mess hall and head straight back to their barracks. Once inside, the recruits stand around as Sergeant O'Toole looks at the lads and remarks, "Each day after Supper, we regroup here. This is where I'll instruct and inform you on Basic Combat Training." All eyes are on the Sergeant. The man continues, "During our evening sessions, we'll go over what needs improvement and prep for upcoming training." The man eyes the group and grins, "Think of it as a Question and Answer time!" Tommy and all the lads nod message received. Sergeant O'Toole strides up and down the barrack's aisle between the bunks, and comments, "Lights out is at 2100 hours. The hour before is Personal Time - you're free to shower, groom, write letters, press your uniform, polish boots, play cards, or just read." The young soldiers glance around with smiles and grins. A guy with red hair remarks with excitement, "YeeHaw! I'm writing my girl back home." Someone at a far bunk quips, "Anyone play Poker?" Another guy yells out, "Texas Hold'em!" All the guys grin and chuckle at the friendly exchange. Sergeant O'Toole walks over and stands beside a central bunk and commands, "Gather round - I'm going to show you the Army Standard for your bunk, cabinet and foot locker." Tommy and his fellow soldiers gather around as the Drill Sergeant demonstrates the correct way to arrange and keep a soldier's bunk, cabinet and foot locker. Tommy keenly watches and makes mental notes of everything the Sergeant does.

# CHAPTER ELEVEN
*Drills and Discipline*

The next day, the first day of Army life, Tommy and his fellow soldiers are up early for 0430 **First Call**, otherwise known as **Reveille**. Sergeant O'Toole begins their **Physical Training** at 0500 hours, putting the troop through energetic calisthenics and running. Tommy's physical conditioning from Ninjan Training enables him to sail through the intense workout. Even though most of his fellow soldiers are healthy young men, they're challenged by the intense early morning Physical Training. The Drill Sergeant puts his troop through their paces, then breaks for **Breakfast** at 0600 hours. The Army style workout has created strong appetites. Tommy and the recruits are hungry and ready to eat a hearty breakfast. Half an hour later at 0630, the **Daily Training** begins and carries on to 1200 for **Lunch**. Tommy and his troop get nourished and re-energized with good nutritious food. At 1230, Sergeant O'Toole continues **Training** until they stop at 1700 hours for **Dinner**. After Tommy and the guys eat their grub, they return to barracks where **Drill Sergeant Time** starts at 1730 hours. During the session, Sergeant O'Toole speaks about important details that fresh recruits face during Basic Training. Tommy listens intently. The time passes quickly as the Drill Sergeant shares his instruction and insight. Soon, it's 2000 hours, Sergeant O'Toole finishes and remarks, "For the first night of BCT, I stay in the barracks with the recruits. For all other nights, I leave the barracks" The recruits eye the Drill Sergeant as he scans around and comments, "The next hour is **Personal Time** - yours to spend it as you like. Dismissed!"

All the recruits disperse to their bunks. Tommy fetches a sheet of paper and envelope and starts a letter to Sarah, writing how he misses and loves her. Throughout the Company barracks, guys are busy with things while others are stretched out to relax. Some get showers, a few start a Poker game, and some guys wash their t-shirts to get rid of the sweat and grime from Physical Training. Mostly everyone is mindful of the remaining moments and finish up in time for **Lights Out** at 2100 hours. All interior lights are switched off, the entire barrack sits dark and still. Tommy stares up at the ceiling, recalling sweet times with Sarah, and former days on the Indian Reservation. Silence lingers across the barracks, the quietness only broken by the intermittent snoring of some very tired recruits. **Day One** is over!

Over the next three weeks, the **Red Phase** of Basic Combat Training begins. The Drill Sergeant takes Tommy and fellow soldiers through intense physical and mental challenges - long distance runs, obstacle courses, field exercise, and demanding drills. Tommy and his company march in company formation, rappel from tall heights, acquire survival skills, and learn First Aid. Company members are also taught small unit tactics (SUT). During the third week of Basic Training, Sergeant O'Toole introduces Tommy and recruits to the standard-issue **M16A2** and the **M4** military rifles. The Officer trains the recruits in how to handle, dismantle, clean, and reassemble their M16A2 and M4A1 military rifles. Tommy's prior mechanical and technical skill, serves him well as he takes apart and reassembles the M16A2 and M4A1 in record fashion. Sergeant O'Toole takes special note of Tommy, recognizing his physical strength, athletic ability, endurance during obstacle courses, his technical skill with military equipment, his quick and intelligent mind, and especially, Tommy's positive attitude toward service and his respect for superiors. The Drill Sergeant places Tommy's name on a special list for new recruits highly recommended for **AIT - Advanced Individual Training**.

The next part of Basic Training the recruits face is the **White Phase** which lasts for three weeks. At the Weapons Range, The Drill Sergeant instructs his young soldiers in marksmanship as they shoot targets on the firing Range. The targets are placed further and further away to develop and sharpen the recruit's marksmanship. Sergeant O'Toole introduces his company to various military weapons and operation. Tommy and fellow recruits learn to use the **M67** Grenade and the **M203** Grenade Launcher, and fire the **M240**, **M249**, and the **M2** Machine guns. Sergeant O'Toole instructs on weaponry characteristics, live fire scenarios, and potential problems that can be encountered in the field with each of the soldier's weapons. Tommy keeps his eyes and ears open, listening intently as Sergeant O'Toole shares his military knowledge acquired from years of training US Military soldiers. Over this White Phase, Tommy and his fellow recruits become skilled and proficient regarding their weapons.

The final stage of Basic Training is the **Blue Phase** that covers a duration of four weeks. The company has to undergo the demanding **APFT - Army Physical Fitness Test**. During each of the previous two phases of basic training, a form of the APFT was conducted on the recruits to ensure the soldiers are in good physical form. However, all recruits will now have to face the full intense challenge of the APFT. Soldiers who do not pass the requirements cannot continue with their platoon. A couple recruits are not successful and have leave the group. Tommy's previous Ninjan training allows him to sail through the rigours and challenges of the APFT - Tommy passes with flying colours. It's during this phase that Sergeant O'Toole takes his soldiers camping, otherwise known as **Bivouac**. There they learn to set up an Army tent, strike camp, and eat the **MRE** (Meal Ready to Eat). Over the course of upcoming days and nights, Tommy and company undergo **Field Training Exercise - FTX**. Sergeant O'Toole gives the young soldiers experience in nighttime combat operations, and leads them through **MOUT - Military Operations in Urban Terrain.** Tommy pays close attention to the Drill Sergeant's orders and instruction. The MOUT component is especially designed to equip soldiers for modern urban warfare, where they fight the enemy house-to-house and street —by-street. Close-quarter combat is decisive as it is extremely dangerous. Events and scenarios can turn in an instant, soldiers must be ready for every type of situation. It's during the second week of this phase, that Military Instructors allow Platoon leaders, like Tommy, to make decisions regarding unit tactics and military strategy. Sergeant O'Toole is there to supervise, but the main purpose, is to develop military leadership.

When it all comes to an end, the final week is known as **Recovery Week.** This is where the recruits must repair and service any of their military gear that's been damaged. The recruits also clean and prepare the barracks for the next group of incoming recruits. An important part of this final phase is when the recruit is fitted for the **Dress Uniform** for Military Graduation. Tommy stands still as a Corporal takes

Tommy's measurements. He reflects back to when the bus arrived on the Army Base, and those first weeks of Red Phase. Tommy looks in the mirror with a contented smile, he's proud to be graduating as a Soldier in the United States Army!

# CHAPTER TWELVE
*Recruit Graduation Ceremony*

# FAMILY DAY

The Army Base is extra busy with the arrival of family and relatives to attend the Family Day and Graduation Ceremony for the recruits. Carl and Sarah flew all the way from home to help celebrate this special occasion. Tommy and his fellow recruits are thrilled to be able to spend time with their loves ones. The Military Brass have arranged venues to make Family Day important and memorable. Throughout the day, recruits take their relatives on tours of the vast army base. For nearly everyone, this is the first time that parents, siblings and fiancees, have been able to see an Army Base in person, up close and behind the scenes. During the day, food and refreshments, are served to the visiting families and recruits. The Army Leadership making sure all the necessary details are looked after. As Tommy escorts Carl and Sarah around the army base, Carl especially likes seeing the Army vehicles, weaponry, and high-tech equipment. Sarah hasn't let go of Tommy's hand since she arrived. Even as Tommy points out equipment features to Carl, he holds onto Sarah's hand like glue. The two love birds are inseparable. Sarah keeps her gaze on Tommy as she gets use to seeing him with a military buzz cut. In her mind's eye, she recalls Tommy's long thick shoulder length shiny black hair. The contrast is startling - yet Sarah is very pleased, because the Army buzz cut lets Tommy's handsome features stand out even more. Sarah squeezes her beau's hand as the three of them walk toward the hanger that house the Black Hawk helicopters. Carl is super delighted to have opportunity to inspect the warcraft inside and out. The old man marvels at the sophisticated hi-tech avionics, the marvellous aeronautical engineering, and the weaponry - the 20mm cannons, the mounted missiles, rockets, and machine guns. Carl is thoroughly impressed. He leans in to get Tommy's ear, "You know, I've always wanted to see one of these! (He looks at his grandson) Thanks Tommy!" The young soldier clasps his grandfather's arm and replies, "I'm so happy that you and Sarah with me today!" Tommy still holding Sarah's hand, motions toward a hanger where crowds of people have gathered outside, "I think it's time for the important afternoon event." Sarah looks into Tommy's eyes and asks, "What important event?" Tommy glances at Carl and Sarah, smiles and replies, "The Military Brass allow the visiting family to pin the Army Infantry Blue Cord on the soldier's right shoulder. (Pause) It's called Turning Blue - when the graduating recruit is officially recognized as an Infantry Soldier of the United States Army!" Carl and Sarah smile widely. Tommy tugs on Sarah's hand and remarks, "We better get over there - I need to join my company and form up for Parade." At those words, the three walk toward the open doors of the big hanger with bleachers and viewing stand in place. Many family members have already got seats in the bleachers, awaiting the Ceremony to unfold. As they near the Hanger pavement, Tommy looks to Sarah and Carl to comment, "You go find a place to sit. I have to be with my unit." Tommy watches as Carl and Sarah find their seats. He remarks quickly, "See you soon." With that, Tommy turns and goes directly through the hanger doors, and disappears from sight.

## TURNING BLUE

Carl and Sarah, and families of the other recruits, watch as Army Brass gather and take chairs on the raised viewing platform. The stirring music of a military band heightens the event as a special occasion to witness and behold. In front of the seated Military Leaders, platoons of soldiers in military dress uniform begin to position on the wide tarmac surface. Bouquets of flowers, celebration ribbons and streamers, decorate the viewing stand and bleachers, marking the event with the patriotic colours of the Red, White, and Blue. Large American flags hang from high above the Hanger doors. Sarah turns to Carl, "This is so exciting!" The old man smiles with a twinkle in his eye, "I'm so proud of Tommy and what he's done!" Carl looks at Sarah, "We have a United Sates Soldier in the family!" Sarah smiles with a girlish giggle, "And I have a United States Soldier for my sweetheart!" The two turn their gaze to what's happening out front, as platoons of soldiers in pristine dress uniform, march with military precision to take positions on the pavement. Carl and Sarah focus their eyes to get a glimpse of Tommy. Sarah grabs Carl's hand and exclaims as she points, "There he is - at the front of the group over there!" Tommy is the Unit Leader and marches out front to lead his unit. Tommy and fellow graduates manoeuvre with synchronized steps in military precision - marching, turning, and positioning alongside the other soldiers mustered on the tarmac. The Military Leaders watch the assembled soldiers, carefully observing the well-formed ranks, the clean crisp uniforms, shiny brass buttons, polished boots, and the faces of strong healthy young men. The presiding Officers are pleased with the young soldiers at attention before them. As the Military Band finishes the last notes of a rousing Military March, a Two Star General stands up, approaches the microphone, turns his gaze to the viewing stand of invited guests, "Welcome to each and every family member, relative and friend on this important day! Assembled before us - are the recruits that have successfully graduated from Basic Combat Training! (Pause) You gave us your sons, grandsons, nephews, brothers, and for some gals - their sweethearts! (The General stands proud) On this day, this Graduation Day, the Army gives back to you - highly trained, dynamic, disciplined, combat capable - Infantry Soldiers of the United States Army!" (Applause! Cheers!) As our Invited Guests, and Family Members of these Graduates, it will be your distinct honour and privilege to pin the Blue Cord that will Identify your graduate as - an Infantry Soldier of the United States Army!" Family members in the bleachers erupt with loud CHEERS and APPLAUSE! The General waits a bit then continues, "As you leave the bleachers, Army Personnel will give each family their Blue Cord, upon which, those family members will seek out their graduate - and proudly pin the Blue Cord on the right shoulder of the soldier. (The General salutes the graduates) Troops Dismissed!" With those official words from the General, the straight rows of young men disperse, and all the graduates make way toward their family, who are leaving the viewing section and spreading out on the Parade Ground. As recruits and family connect - there are hugs, tears, big proud smiles, and kisses from Sweethearts. Across the Parade Ground, individual pockets form as graduates and their families huddle together. The distinct privilege of who will perform the Graduation Ritual varies; in one family it's the Father, for another family it's the Mother, for one graduate an older Brother will perform the honour, for another young man - his

Grandfather will assist. Every graduate seems so mature, no longer the awkward young kid from before, now, they stand tested and trained. Carl and Sarah find Tommy amid the throng of uniformed young men. The trio stand close together, around them are open spaces that separate the various family units scattered across the tarmac. Sarah looks at Tommy and tears well up in her eyes - she remembers the first time they met as teenagers at the Gold Eagle Dojo, Tommy was so awkward, so unsure, so undisciplined. Now, standing before her, is a strong disciplined handsome soldier in uniform. Sarah reaches out to hug and kiss Tommy. As Sarah steps back, Tommy turns his gaze to his Grandfather. Carl stands tall, his face beams with pride, his hand holds the Blue Cord. Tommy looks at Sarah and Carl, and he humbly requests, "Grandfather! I'd like you to pin the Blue Cord under my right lapel and under my right shoulder, please!" The Grandfather with moist eyes, pins the Blue Cord on Tommy's uniform. When Carl pulls away his arms, Tommy glances down at the Blue Cord on his right shoulder. He is momentarily transfixed. Sarah remarks, "It looks special!" Tommy replies with a smile. "Sweetheart, it is special! I'm no longer just a recruit - Officially, I'm an Infantry Soldier of the Unites States Army!" Carl pats Tommy's back and comments, "You did it, Tommy! I knew when you enlisted that you'd reach this day. Congratulations!" Tommy reaches into his trouser pocket to bring out the Token, and remarks, "Grandpa, I kept your Token with me through it all!" Carl smiles and replies, "Now you carry two honours. You wear the Infantry Blue Cord, and you carry the Ninjan Token of Honour!" Tommy grins, "Guess I'm doubly blessed!" Sarah gives a playful poke and quips, "Hey, Triple blessed! What about me?!" Tommy reaches out to hug Sarah and swing her in circles. Carl, Tommy and Sarah are laughing and smiling. All around them, other families are celebrating with their young men, their important Military milestone - Turning Blue!

As the eventful day comes to a close, it is time for all civilians, the invited family members, to leave the Army Base. The new Infantry Soldiers bid farewell as their families get into the parked vehicles that were permitted on the Base by special invitation. Tommy walks Sarah and Carl to the rental car and gives Sarah a parting kiss. He looks at the car and remarks, "It's nice your flight included a car rental." Carl opens the driver's door and gets seated behind the steering wheel, "We drop it off at the Airport - then catch our flight back home (gazes at grandson) Tommy - it sure has been an outstanding day! I'm so proud of you - and so proud to be a part of your Graduation!" Tommy lowers down and looks through the window at Carl and Sarah, "You made all the difference - Thank you for being here today!" As Carl starts the engine, Tommy steps back away from the car, eyes Sarah and winks, "Love you Hon!" Sarah blows Tommy a kiss, "Love you my handsome soldier!" Tommy grins and loudly exclaims, "HOORAH!" He backs up and watches the car pull away and move toward the Main Gate.

# CHAPTER THIRTEEN
## *Advanced Individual Training*

With Basic Combat Training now complete, Tommy and his fellow Infantry Soldiers, enter the next stage known as **AIT - Advanced Individual Training**. AIT prepares soldiers for their **MOS - Military Occupational Specialty**. Once a soldier selects a MOS, that is where the soldier will serve during their military career. MOS can vary from - Army Corps of Engineers, Electronics and Telecommunications, Administration, Medical; to that of Infantry, Ordinances, Military Police, and Intelligence. Tommy has elected to remain with Infantry and choose Reconnaissance as his MOS. In Tommy's mind, Surveillance and Scouting territory fits well with his American Indian heritage. After all, that is exactly what his Tribe's forefathers did centuries before, as their people travelled to various hunting and fishing grounds. Now, as an Infantry Army Soldier, he can use Recon knowledge and skills to better serve his country. Tommy's prior Ninjan training for Stealth, Camouflage, and Concealment will be of immense help when working Recon. The combination of advanced military training and Ninjan skills will give Tommy the benefits of both worlds. No one at the Army base is aware of his Ninjan skills and expertise; not his Drill Sergeant, none of his fellow soldiers, nor any of the high ranking Military Brass. On the outside, Tommy simply looks like an American Indian, who is an Infantry Soldier in the US Army; little would anyone suspect that Tommy is a Ninjan Master, an expert in Ninja skills and weapons. Tommy's Army discipline, and his gentle demeanour, hide the fact he is probably the most lethal soldier on Base.

Master Sergeant Powers is Tommy's AIT Platoon Sergeant. He's a lean, fit, tough-as-nails soldier. O'Toole speaks to Powers on Tommy's success during the Basic Combat Training phase. Sergeant O'Toole hands Powers an olive-coloured military file and comments, "He's the best I've seen in a long time! Great skills. Great potential." The Master Sergeant opens the folder, peruses Tommy's information, then remarks, "I'll keep my eye on him. If he's as good as you say - there's a perfect place for him!" Sergeant O'Toole asks, "What place is that?" Sergeant Powers quips, "Army Recon!" Sergeant O'Toole smiles and blurts out, "HOORAH!"

The Advanced Individual Training program is far more demanding and intense that what Tommy experienced with Basic Combat Training. Sergeant Powers is a strict taskmaster who believes in pushing soldiers to reach their maximum potential. Tommy and fellow soldiers are pushed to navigate complex obstacle courses, crawl under barbwire with live fire flying overhead, scale imposing log walls, and perform rock climbing in full battle gear with backpack. The day-to-day training in enough to challenge strong young men. Back at the Barracks, Tommy and the others nurse - bruises, sore muscles, scraps, and aching joints. Over time, Sergeant Powers notices the improved fitness and stamina exhibited by Tommy. It was during one of the obstacle courses over rough terrain in full battle gear, that the Master Sergeant spotted Tommy way out in front of the others straining to keep up. At the end of the obstacle run, when the others have collapsed and buckled with exhaustion, Tommy stood strong and tall in his battle gear. As Sergeant Powers approached, Tommy saluted, and Powers remarked, "Looks like you're the only one left standing!" Tommy gives a soldierly gaze and replies, "Ripped and ready, Master Sergeant!" The older man scans around at the others regaining their wind, and comments, "Appears your unit needs improvement!" Tommy stares ahead at Attention, and remarks, "The unit will get better, Master Sergeant! Stronger and Better. Sir!" The Master Sergeant eyes Tommy and replies, "I'm making you Platoon Unit Leader - effective immediately!" Tommy salutes and yells in response, "I'll do my best, Master Sergeant!" Powers comments as he walks away, "I know you will, soldier! I know you will". By this time, all the platoon soldiers are back on their feet and ready for the Master Sergeant's next order. Powers scans the group and barks with a grin, "Double-Time back to the Barracks! Move it!" Tommy and the troops jump to and hustle back double-time to the Barracks — just in time for Chow.

Over the succeeding weeks and months at Infantry School, Tommy and fellow soldiers become highly skilled regarding - Weapons and Vehicle Operation, Land Reconnaissance, Map Reading, Navigation, Minefields, constructing Barriers and Fighting Positions, and operating Communication Equipment. A vital requirement for Tommy is to attend the US Army Airborne School (also known as Jump School). There, he is trained to be a Paratrooper, an effective military parachutist. Jump School prepares soldiers with the ability to go into the field, day or night, foreign or domestic, through airborne operations.

The result of rigorous training and instruction from Military Experts, installs warfare strategy and battle readiness in Tommy and company. From a fledgling new recruit who had to be taught to march, Tommy is now a skilled Infantryman; capable of handling weapons, vehicles, avoid mines, use military radio, scout enemy terrain, and establish firefight positions. Tommy has become a formidable Military Warrior!

# CHAPTER FOURTEEN

*Orders From Superiors*

The sun shines overhead on the Army Base during the Platoon's afternoon Combat Drill. The Master Sergeant has paired up soldiers on the exercise field to spar and demonstrate combat skills and fighting technique. Tommy's opponent is Derek, a big strong 6 foot 4 inch guy of Swedish background. Derek seems to tower over Tommy. The guys in the Platoon watch as the pair face each other. Sergeant Powers tosses the wooden Ka-Bar military knife to Derek, points at Tommy and orders, "Attack him!" As Derek lumbers forward, Tommy moves side to side, as he keeps his eyes on the big brute coming to attack. Derek picks an opportunity and lunges with the training knife at Tommy's midsection. But Tommy is too quick and turns sideways to avoid contact. Derek attacks again. This time, as Derek swipes the blade, Tommy grabs the big guy's arm, wrenches his wrist to make Derek drop the knife. Derek gets frustrated and throws a punch, which Tommy blocks. Dereks straightens up, makes a face, then sends out a big kick. Tommy tilts to dodge the kick, grabs Derek's leg at the heel and pulls upward. The leg goes high in the air, Derek loses his balance and falls backwards onto the ground. At this stage, Sergeant Powers and all the Platoon have their eyes glued to what's happening. Derek raises his head off the ground and looks at everyone watching him. He feels embarrassed! Derek gets back on his feet and runs to grab and throttle his opponent. Tommy catches Derek's arm, torques and spins Derek around, locking him into a submission hold. Derek struggles to get free but can't - after a vain attempt - Derek taps out. Tommy lets Derek go and the big guy looks at Tommy and remarks, "Where did you learn that stuff?" Tommy replied, "My Grandfather taught me Martial Arts!" With the whole Platoon's eyes still on the two combatants, Sergeant Powers strides up to Tommy, "Good combat skills, soldier!" Tommy salutes, "Thank You Sir!" The Master Sergeant glances at Derek and the others, then comments, "This only goes to show - that size doesn't always matter! When you use your combat skills (eyes Derek) you can defeat bigger foes!" The Officer scans the group and barks, "Keep on training! (Motions arm) Let's have another set of combatants!" With that, Powers steps away as another pair of soldiers move into the middle and get ready to fight. Tommy stands in the Platoon's perimeter observing the combatants, when Derek approaches and positions beside him. Tommy glances over and Derek quietly asks, "Do you think you can show me some of those moves?" Tommy grins and remarks, "You got it, Derek! Be glad to show you a few tricks." The big guy grins and relies, "Great! I sure don't want any repeat of today!" Tommy and Derek nod and smile as they both watch the combat match before them.

The Army Program of **OSUT - One Station Unit Training** - combines Basic Combat Training and Advanced Individual Training to take place at the same location. For Tommy, he receives all his MOS training at the same Army Base. As an Infantryman, Tommy works his path toward becoming a Calvary Scout, a soldier highly trained to scout and survey terrain, identify enemy positions, evaluate opposing military equipment and firepower, and communicate with Command regarding troop advance or withdraw. In the field, Tommy is exceptional and performs with excellence and skill. The Military Instructors are very impressed with Tommy's seeming natural ability to excel as a Calvary Scout. Such a role is no "walk-in-the-park", as a Calvary Scout, Tommy had to work alone and be exposed to the brunt of nature's elements - the hot sun, cold nights, heavy rains, blowing wind, all the while trekking and climbing rugged terrain and dense forest. Only once did Tommy have an issue, and that wasn't of his making - the electronic equipment had a faulty switch which stopped radio communication. Not to be deterred, Tommy got within sight of the Command post and he used his tactical flashlight to send the information via morse code. To say the least, the Field Instructors were greatly impressed at Tommy's resolve and ingenuity!

Near the end of OSUT Training, Master Sergeant Powers approaches Tommy with specific orders. Tommy stands at ease as Sergeant Powers remarks, "Major Strikklan wants to see you!" Tommy salutes his Platoon Sergeant and promptly replies, "Yes Sir!" At delivering the message, Sergeant Powers and Tommy make their way to the Officers' Building, enter within and stand outside Major Strikklan's open door. The Sergeant knocks to announce his presence with a salute, "Sergeant Powers, Sir! Infantryman Long Grass as you requested." The Major looks up from the open folders on his desk, salutes back and remarks, "Thank you Master Sergeant! That will be all. Dismissed." Sergeant Powers salutes, pivots about and leaves to go down the hall. The Major extends his hand to the empty chair before the desk and comments, "Soldier. Please take a seat." Tommy salutes, enters the office, quickly looks around, then sits down in the chair and with eyes straight ahead. The Major gives a slight smile and asks a question to test, " Without looking around - what can you tell me about my office?" Tommy makes eye contact with Major Strikklan and replies, "Hidden by the open door, you have a set of golf clubs, - behind me on the wall, there's a Military Graduation photo, you're in the second row on the left, - your office had a small leak, your ceiling tile has the faded signs of water damage, - and you have 8 folders on your desk." Major Strikklan is clearly impressed. He counts the folders 1...2...3......8, then fixes his gaze on Tommy, smiles and comments, "Great job soldier! That's exactly what I'd expect of an Army Calvary Scout - a soldier who can identify and analyze his environment." Tommy replies, "Thank you Sir!" The Officer leans back in his chair as he observes Tommy for a couple moments, then he comments, "Tommy, (Major opens a file) both Sergeant O'Toole and Sergeant Powers have given you high recommendations. You're presently trained as a Calvary Scout (Pause) How would you like to join the Army's Special Forces and do Special Reconnaissance?" Tommy's eyes widen at hearing the Major's words, and he sits quiet. Major Strikklan understands the situation and gives Tommy a couple minutes to reflect upon what's been said. The Major picks up Tommy's file and peruses some paperwork, puts down the folder and remarks, "You passed BCT, AIT, and Jump School with flying colours. Your Field Instructors gave you high marks... from the looks of things, you're perfectly suited for Army **Special Reconnaissance**. (Looks at Tommy) That's what I'm offering you - the opportunity and privilege to join the **US Army's Special Operation Forces**! (Pause) what's your reply?" Tommy reflects for a second, then breaks out in a big smile and a positive response, "Yes Sir! Thank you Sir! It would be an honour to serve as Special Forces in the Army!" Major Stikklan places Tommy's folder into a desk tray marked **APPROVED**, stands up and extends his arm to Tommy,

"Congratulations Tommy! Welcome to the Special Forces of the United States Army!" Tommy stands at Attention, shakes the Major's hand, salutes and replies, "Thank You Sir! **Special Forces! HOORAH!**" The Major smiles at the enthusiasm and eagerness displayed by Tommy. Major Stikkan salutes Tommy and replies with a firm smile, "You will train at an Army Base in another State. I will send your file to Master Sergeant Powers. He will inform you of all the details. Dismissed soldier." Tommy smiles, salutes Major Stikklan, pivots about, exits the office and walks down the corridor. Tommy's face shines full of pride and purpose.

# CHAPTER FIFTEEN

## *Special Operations Force*

As Tommy's military career advances, he finds himself in a different State in the warm American southeast. The Army Base has stellar programs, facilities, and expert instructors; that school, train, test, and prepare soldiers to be Army Special Operations Forces. The soldiers are schooled in Advanced Special Operations Techniques (ASOT), Interagency Operations, and (SERE) Survival, Evasion, Resistance and Escape.

Tommy and fellow warriors receive military training to carry out - direct action, unconventional warfare, foreign internal defence, special Reconnaissance, and military strategy for combating terrorism. The most challenging part for anyone is the gruelling **Special Forces Qualification Course (SFQC)**, simply known as "Q Course". Phase 1 is 13 weeks long, where candidates are extremely tested, and only the soldiers who are successful become accepted and approved. Tommy endures the crucible of testing and qualifies for further elite military training. He enters Phase 2, where for another 13 weeks, the young man learns and practices Small Unit Tactics (SUT) and Operations. He acquires battle-ready combat skills that are a hallmark of Special Forces. Tommy successfully completes all stages of the Special Forces Qualification Course, and he graduates as a Special Forces soldier, and is assigned to a 12-man Operational Detachment "A" (ODA), otherwise known as "A Team".

In the Barracks that house his ODA, with Lights Out and all quiet, Tommy lays on his bunk still awake not ready to sleep. His mind wanders back to life on the Indian Reservation of Venture, to the noisy Auto Shop with cars on hoists, to romantic times with his beautiful sweetheart Sarah, and deeply smiles at how they dated, danced, snugged - and kissed. Tommy thinks of Grandpa Carl and sessions of Ninjan training. The young man recalls how he and Carl sparred with the Katana swords, practiced hand-to-hand combat, threw Shuriken stars at targets, and listened as Carl spoke of his beloved Japanese culture. Tommy shifts his head on the pillow and stretches out to get more comfortable. All those memories seem so long ago. Tommy reflects back on his arrival at the Military Base, his progress through BCT, AIT, Jump School, and the demanding Q Course. He lifts his arm to place it behind his head on the pillow, the position helps his body to relax more. Tommy reflects on the military weapons he's capable of using - the M16A2 and M4A1 combat rifles, the M67 Grenade and M203 Grenade Launcher, the M240, M249, and the M2 Machine guns. He can drive a Humvee and Armoured Troop Carrier, Rappel into buildings for Hostage Rescue, Parachute and Survive behind Enemy Lines, execute Close Quarter Combat, Field Dress injuries on the battle field, and conduct Special Reconnaissance.

Tommy's eyes are feeling heavy and he yawns as his body gets tired. He's ready for sleep. The young man pulls up the cover with a contented smile and closes his eyes. Tommy is very pleased and deeply proud to serve as a US Army Special Forces Soldier!

# CHAPTER SIXTEEN
## *ODA - Operational Detachment Alphas*

With the 12-man ODA unit, a close bond exists for the "Brothers in Arms" - after all, their very lives depend on each other. Tommy realizes the importance of such camaraderie and takes steps to foster greater ties with his fellow warriors. Members of the unit are from all over - the deep south, Louisiana and Texas - the industrial north, Michigan and New York, - the American heartland, Wisconsin and Iowa, - the Pacific Coast, California and Oregon, - the Southwest, Arizona and New Mexico. Only one other member hails from the Northwest, Montana, whereas, Tommy is from Wyoming. These elite Special Forces soldiers are literally from all across the country, and that's especially fitting, since these Army soldiers represent the United States of America!

As Special Forces, Tommy and his unit, continue with field training and military class instruction. The ODA Unit constantly exercise with calisthenics, weights, and long distance running, to keep fit and stay strong. The soldiers practice specialized warfare, combat scenarios during the day, and high risk operations in the dark with night-vision goggles. Tommy's role on the "A" Team is Special Reconnaissance (SR). His military training combined with his secret Ninjan skills makes Tommy exceptionally unique at Recon. He's in top athletic form, an expert in stealth and camouflage, possessing excellent Surveillance skills, and having razor-sharp battle instincts, Tommy is truly perfect for Special Forces Recon!

# CHAPTER SEVENTEEN
## *On Foreign Soil*

It happened on a somewhat regular day, as the ODA Unit were practicing their specialized skills when the Order came from Military Superiors - Immediate Deployment Overseas.

Tommy and Unit members gather their battle gear and specialized weapons, and get loaded on the Military aircraft for the flight overseas. The ODA Team Leader carries the sealed Priority 1 Orders dispatched from Army Command. As Tommy and team members look on, the Captain unseals the envelope and communicates the Military Directive - HOSTAGE RESCUE. AFGHANISTAN. HINDU KUSH MOUNTAINS. All eyes are on the Captain as he scans the Orders and remarks, "Three American NGOs, two females and one male, have been kidnapped by a rogue Warlord, and being kept for Ransom. Command has given the GPS Coordinates where the captives are being held." The Captain scans around at his men and declares, "This is a Priority Extraction - Not Seek and Destroy. I repeat - Not Seek and Destroy!" Tommy and fellow warriors nod acknowledgement to their Unit Leader. The man folds up the Order, unzips his Combat Vest and puts away the paper. The Military aircraft flies very high in the upper atmosphere, so strong winds can help the plane make better time to their destination. Tommy and group try to grab some shut-eye and rest up to reserve their energy for the Mission. The afternoon sun is setting on the horizon when the Military airplane sets down on the runway at the massive Bagram Air Base, situated just over 6 miles southeast of Charikar in the Parwan Province of Afghanistan. After the Aircraft taxis to its designated location, Tommy's ODA Unit quickly exit the Cargo plane and transfer to two Blackhawk Helicopters with propellors rotating - ready for Take-Off. The  soldiers have practiced this maneuver many times, the 12-man unit split apart as each 6-man team load into a Blackhawk. With the Special Forces soldiers onboard and official clearance from the Air Base Control Tower - the two Blackhawks lift off and head out in a Northeast direction. The navigation lights glow in the night sky as the Blackhawks fly silently over the Afghan mountain terrain. On board the helicopters, each ODA 6-Man Team preps for action, checking weapons, tactical gear, and donning their night-vision goggles. Tommy sits in quiet confidence, battle-ready for action.

The Blackhawks quietly land on flat sandy ground, dotted with wilderness shrubs and tuffs of tall grass, just a 1/2 Click out from the target area. The ODA Unit gather for a quick huddle to synchronize watches, 'lock and load' weapons, double check combat gear, and activate the night vision goggles. The soldiers stand alert with weapons ready. The Captain speaks, "We travel in on foot. 1000 yards out - Tommy and Team will scope out with 'eyes and ears' on the Compound. (Turns to Tommy) You Recon exactly where the 3 hostages are being held. When Intel is confirmed - We go in!" The Captain looks at his men, "Copy that?" The entire group nod affirmative! With the ODA Unit on the same page, the soldiers head out, their night vision googles enable them to navigate the rough ground. In a short time, the ODA soldiers stop 1000 yards out from the cluster of brick and earthen buildings that sit enclosed by an earthen wall 4 feet high. With the other Unit members at the ready, Tommy and his Team scurry to the perimeter wall, and duck low to stay hidden. As his Team members scope out the compound in all directions, Tommy slips over the wall and sneaks to the buildings nearby. The soldiers on his Team keep Tommy in their rifle scopes, their triggers ready to deal with anyone that posses a threat. Their Special Forces M4A1 rifles with Silencers can produce a quiet deadly kill. Tommy quickly moves from one building to another - peering in - gathering Intel, then moving to the next building. At the fourth building, Tommy peeks in through a crack in the wood shutter. He sees two females and one male, gagged and tied to interior wood posts. Tommy looks closer - the hostages appear tired and exhausted from their ordeal, but healthy and alive! Just as Tommy turns his face away from the shutter, he hears the crunch of boots on the ground nearby. He looks around to see two of the Warlord's fighters confronting him. The two fighters draw out razor sharp Kukuri knives. Tommy waves the hand signal to "Hold Off". In the blink of an eye, Tommy swiftly strikes both fighters, pummelling their bodies with repeated blows to disable and drop them to the ground. The Kukuri knives lay in the dirt. Tommy quickly sprints back over the wall, and his team rejoin the other ODA members. The Captain looks and Tommy remarks, "The hostages are gagged and tied up in the fourth building. (Tommy points at Compound Diagram). I knocked out two guards. We need to move now!" The Captain signals and all the soldiers quietly make haste to the perimeter wall. Hunkered down at the wall, the Leader instructs, "Tommy and Team will free the hostages. We will cover them!" As the soldiers direct their M4A1 rifles toward the buildings, Tommy and team hustle over the wall and quickly go to the fourth building where the two fighters still lay unconscious on the dusty ground. As three members keep watch, Tommy and two soldiers enter the interior. At first, the hostages are alarmed and scared at the sudden intrusion - the flickering light of the kerosene lamps only partially light the interior. But when Tommy and his fellow soldiers reach the hostages, they become relaxed and relieved to see the United States Flag front and centre on the Special Forces' uniform. Tommy and comrades loosen the gags and cut the plastic ties that bind the hostages' arms and legs. One of the gals looks bewildered from shock, Tommy comments, "US Army Special Forces - We're here to rescue you and take you home!" The hostages are physically tired from the stress and strain of their captivity, Tommy and the two soldiers help the hostages toward the door. Once outside the structure, the 6-man Team help the hostages to reach and clear the perimeter wall. With weapons trained on the Compound as cover, the ODA soldiers assist the freed captives over the rugged terrain away from the Compound. Each of the hostages holds onto the shoulder of the soldier in front of them, the night-vision goggles allow the soldiers to safely guide them where to walk. Reaching the GPS coordinates for Extraction, Tommy and the ODA Unit watch. In a matter of 90 seconds, the quiet whirl of propellors can be heard - then the blast of wind as the Blackhawk helicopters land. The soldiers and hostages shield their eyes and mouths as they move toward the open side doors of aircraft. Each 6-Man Team return to the Blackhawk they rode in - the only joyful exception being the 3 American NGO hostages joining them for the ride to Freedom. The Blackhawks lift off quiet as a whisper, and soon both aircraft are flying high, heading back to the Air Base. On board, the two girls and the young guy, rejoice at being rescued and set free - tears of joy run down their soot-covered faces as they have big smiles of relief. Tommy and his fellow soldiers rest proud and content, knowing they successfully carried out their Mission to rescue the hostages - with no loss of life!

When they reach Bagram Air Base, the hostages are taken care of by Army medical personnel and staff from the American Diplomatic Corps. The Special Forces soldiers have earned some well-deserved R & R, so they get soothing hot showers and enjoy some quality 'Down Time'. The next day, Tommy's ODA Unit catch a Military plane back to the US and they return to their home Army Base. Once back in their Unit Barracks, the ODA Unit meet with Military Superiors to Report and Debrief about the Rescue Mission. Tommy's Unit learn later on, that one of the volunteer GNO females is the daughter of someone very high up in the American Government. The reason Tommy and the ODA Unit conducted the Mission is because of two main reasons - 1. They are Special Forces soldiers carrying out Military Orders, and - 2. The hostages were Americans. - America takes care of its own!

# CHAPTER EIGHTEEN

*Special Instructor - Weapons Master Sergeant*

Tommy's military career is bright and promising. Military Superiors have recognized Tommy's excellent record of Army Service - taking note of his outstanding progress through BCT, AIT, Jump School, Q Course, - and his success as a member of the Special Forces ODA Team. The Army Military Brass have given Tommy the position of Corporal. One afternoon, Major Strikklan sends for Tommy to be in his Office. Tommy makes his way to the Officers' Building and stands outside Major Strikklan's open door. Tommy knocks to announce his presence. As Major Strikklan looks up, Tommy salutes and speaks, "Corporal Long Grass reporting as ordered, Sir!" The Officer smiles and waves his hand in a friendly gesture, "Come in, Corporal, and take a seat." Tommy enters and sits down in the chair opposite the Officer. Major Strikklan opens a drawer and pulls out a military file folder, peruses the contents, sets the folder down on the desk in front of him, looks at Tommy and remarks, "Your Military File indicates you're being Promoted to the rank of Sergeant." Tommy blinks at the news and promptly replies, "Thank You, Sir! Always ready to serve!" The Officer smiles, happy to know that Tommy's zeal and commitment for Army Serve has not diminished over time. Major Strikklan leans forward, clasps his hands and enquires in an almost fatherly tone, "Corporal, where would you like to serve in the Army? (Pause) What MOS Classification are you interested in?" Tommy smiles wide and gives a positive response, "Sir, I'd like to serve as MOS 18 BRAVO - Special Forces Weapons Sergeant, Sir!" Major Strikklan opens the folder to peruse content details, then lifts his head with a firm smile, "From your Record - it appears you would do very well in the role as a MOS 18B!" Tommy sits firm and alert, and replies, "Thank You for your confidence, Sir!" The Major fills in some blank spots on a Military

Form, places his signature, closes the folder, and comments, "Your new designation of Army MOS 18B will begin in 14 days, commencing at 1200 hours. (The Major Stands and extends arm) Congratulations Sergeant!" Tommy extends his arm and shakes the Major's hand, "Thank You, Sir! Special Forces - HOORAH!" The Major grins and replies, "That's all soldier. Dismissed!" As the Officer sits back into his desk chair, Tommy stands, salutes and pivots about, exits the Major's Office and strides down the hallway, his chest bursting with pride, his face filled with delight.

......14 Days later

At 1200 hours, military time, Master Sergeant Powers goes to see Tommy at the Baracks and brings him a package. The NCO was one of Tommy's mentors, and has now become Tommy's friend, "This is for you Tommy! Go ahead open it!" Powers watches as Tommy unwraps the package to reveal a crisp clean Sergeant's uniform. The older man comments, "You can put away your Corporal uniform and put on your Sergeant uniform! You've earned it!" Tommy smiles and salutes his friend, and Powers salutes back. In a matter of minutes, Tommy has disappeared into a Barrack side room, and soon emerges dressed in his new Special Forces Weapons Sergeant uniform. Tommy strides over sporting a wide smile. He stands admiring his new Sergeant's uniform with Special Forces Insignia, Sergeant Stripes, and Weapons Specialist designation. Powers exclaims, "You look sharp. Real sharp!" Tommy stands proud and pleased. Sergeant Powers eyes Tommy and remarks, "You do know it's Chow at the Mess Hall?" Tommy gives a quick nod and replies with a grin, "We better get some grub before it's all gone!" Sergeant Powers and the newly-minted Weapons Sergeant Long Grass exit the barracks, and make their way to the Army Mess Hall where the Dinner Menu reads - Southern Fried Chicken, Potato Salad, Corn-on-the-Cob, Mixed Vegetables, Fruits, and for Dessert - Pie and Ice Cream. Yum!

In the coming days, weeks, and months, Tommy quickly learns his new Army role. In the Modular Training for a Special Forces Weapons Sergeant, Tommy gains technical knowledge and practical instruction, both on and off the field. He quickly becomes an accomplished Specialist with various types of weapons used by American, European, and Foreign Military. Tommy becomes proficient with weapons that include the M9, Makarov, Browning and Colt pistols, assorted submachine guns, and the M4A1, SKS, G3A4, and AK47 rifles; 60, 80 and 120mm mortars; the anti-tank M136 AT4, and anti-aircraft weapon systems such as the Stinger and Javelin missiles. As a Weapons Specialist, Tommy understands battlefield strategy regarding weapon placement and Arc of Fire, techniques in training US soldiers in weaponry, and how to select, train, and organize foreign forces for the combat theatre. As time goes by and further experience gained, within his Special Forces Operational Detachment Alpha (SFODA), Tommy has become the Senior Weapons Sergeant. The Military Superiors have their eyes on Tommy. He's been on their radar for a while. The Military Brass always like to know their top soldiers!

Over the coming months, the Special Forces ODA Team receives various Overseas Missions that are Priority 1 Operations that are "Classified" on an a "Need To Know" basis. On one assignment, Tommy and fellow warriors protect important foreign oil interests during civil unrest. For another Mission, Tommy and the Junior Weapons Sergeant help train overseas soldiers to combat an illegitimate Coup. However, the Mission that impacted Tommy the most, was the Rescue of young school children from the hands of radical insurgents, who threatened to kill the youngsters. When Tommy saw the freed children and anxious parents run to hug each other, the scene touched Tommy's heart. On the outside, Tommy is a Special Forces soldier, lethal in battle and hardened by the fire of combat; yet inside, he has a tender heart and caring soul. Such is the character and mettle of Senior Weapons Sergeant Tommy Long Grass!

It has been five years, since Tommy first arrived on Base as a new recruit. Now, being a NCO with sterling service and an outstanding record from numerous assignments, Tommy requests Special Leave from his Superiors, to visit back home in the Indian Reservation of Venture. Over the years, this is only the second such request, and one that Tommy is anxious to receive. With approval from Military Brass, Tommy catches a Military plane that will take him to Wyoming. When the flight lands, Tommy is delighted to see Carl at the Main Gate to drive him home. Sarah would have been there to greet her sweetheart, but she had to work because of her Nursing Shift. Tommy holding a short duffle bag, waves to greet Carl and walks out the Army Base Main Gate toward Carl's parked car. Tommy opens the back passenger door, tosses in the duffle bag, then gets seated and buckled up in the passenger front seat. He looks at his Grandfather with a smile, "So nice to see you Grandpa. Thanks for picking me up!" Carl glances at his grandson, "You look bigger than last time I saw you! (Laughs) Must be all that Army food!" They both chuckle. Carl starts the car and the vehicle leaves the Main Gate parking area, and heads toward the State Highway that will take them home to Venture. Along the drive home, as the car goes through the wilderness of rock, shrub and sand; Tommy takes his gaze off the landscape and looks at his Grandfather, "This is a really important visit!" Carl perks up and his eye brows raise - he glances at Tommy and comments, "Sounds serious! What is it?" Tommy responds with a big smile and pulls out a small velvet box from his front pocket, opens it to reveal a sparkling Diamond ring. Carl's eyes widen as he gets a big grin, "You're finally going to do it?" Tommy beams and looks at Carl, "Yes! I'm asking Sarah to marry me! (Slight pause) I hope she says Yes!?" Carl keeps his eyes on the road ahead and comments, "She's been your gal since the Gold Eagle Dojo. You're all she ever talks about!" Tommy turns the ring and stares as the diamond sparkles in the sunlight, "We've been dating since we met at Gold Eagle (takes a breath) I think it's time I propose and make it official - ask for Sarah's hand!" Tommy closes the velvet box and tucks it back in his front pocket, and stares out the windshield, deep in thought. Carl gives a peek over at his grandson and tenderly remarks, "Tommy - you both are made for each other! You know that - and Sarah knows that! That ring will tell people what's already inside the heart - that You love Sarah and Sarah loves you!" Tommy turns his gaze toward Carl and replies, "Thanks Grandpa!" Along the drive, Grandfather and Grandson talk about old times practicing Ninjan skills, what's been happening on the Indian reserve, and Tommy gives an update on his military life. As the car motors down the Highway, Tommy spots local landmarks and he realizes they're getting close to home.

# CHAPTER NINETEEN
*The Big Proposal*

The Chevy Malibu reaches the Indian Reservation of Venture, and Carl and Tommy soon arrive home at the raised brick bungalow on Plains Road. Tommy smiles as he sees his classic blue Mustang safely stored under the canvass tarp. When Carl pulls to a stop and cuts the engine, Tommy remarks, "I'll get the Mustang ready so I can pick up Sarah at the Hospital." Carl comments, "That's great! I'll start supper (eyes Tommy) We're gonna have Lasagna, garlic toast, and garden salad." Tommy grins, "Grandpa - I've always loved your cooking!" The Grandfather shakes his head with a grin, "Yes, I know - I remember as a teenager, you'd pat your tummy and tell me - my food was going to 'Waist'!" The two exit the car and Tommy replies, "And now, I turn all food into muscle!" Tommy playfully pats his muscular six-pack and Carl laughs.

Tommy lifts the canvass tarp off his car, pops the trunk, stores the tarp in the cargo hold, then shuts the lid. Once behind the wheel in the leather driver seat, Tommy starts the engine and smiles at the throaty roar with each rev of the big engine. The young man shifts from Park and Drives the Mustang off the property, onto Plains Road and through the Indian Reserve. Driving past familiar sites and old haunts, memories come flooding back to Tommy. He recalls the early trouble with the Gang, the Court Case and the Judge's Decision for him to live with his Grandparents. Tommy remembers the Gold Eagle Dojo where he first met Sarah, and the way High School got better, and how Grandpa Carl gave him Ninjan training, and finally; the time Carl and Sarah said Good Bye as he got on the Army Bus. Tommy is amazed at all that's taken place in what seems a short time. As the young man drives, he sees the Hospital up ahead. He steers into the Parking Lot and stops at the base of the Main Entrance steps, and waits. Tommy keeps his eyes at the top of the steps - waiting to get a glimpse of his sweetheart. Soon, Sarah exits the Hospital's sliding front glass doors - sees the blue Mustang parked at the base of the steps and jumps for joy with a big smile. Sarah races down the steps, opens the car door and gets inside. She looks at Tommy as if seeing him for the very first time - she leans in to give Tommy a big smooch. The two lover birds are frozen in a romantic lingering kiss. Sarah pulls away and exclaims, "Oh Tommy, I've missed you so much!" Tommy holds Sarah's hand and replies, "Sweetheart, I've really missed you too!" As Sarah does up her seat belt, Tommy comments, "After supper tonight, let's drive to one of our favourite spots - like old times!" Sarah's eyes light up and she replies, "I have just the spot - (big smile) remember where we first kissed?" Tommy grins and responds, "I sure do! (Chuckles) I was so nervous." Sarah counters, "Hey, you weren't the only one - I tried on 5 different lipsticks for that date (winks) I knew we were finally gonna kiss." Tommy starts the engine and pulls away from the building, "Well, we got Grandpa's food waiting for us, after that - a special time just for us!" The young lady reaches out to touch Tommy's hand on the gear shift, "I can't wait!" With Tommy and Sarah once again in the Mustang together, like when they were dating, they head toward home and the delicious meal that Carl has prepared for them. Sarah and Tommy pull onto the property and make their way into the house where Carl has the dining table set with Lasagna, garlic bread, garden salad, a fruit bowl, a pitcher of ice tea, and a Dutch Apple pie. Carl waves the couple over and the three sit down to the appetizing meal.

Later after they finish eating, Sarah bids Carl sit and relax as she and Tommy clear the table and wash the dishes. Carl goes to the recliner, puts his feet up, and flips open the local newspaper. Tommy and Sarah clear the dining table and wash and put away the plates, cutlery, glasses, pots and pans. With everything tidied up in the kitchen and the dining table wiped clean, Sarah looks at Tommy and remarks, "I'll freshen up!" Tommy responds, "I'll sit with Grandpa until you're ready." Sarah takes her purse and goes into the spare bedroom, while Tommy goes to sit on the sofa near Carl reading the paper.

The evening is just setting in as they leave the house. Sarah has freshened up her makeup and wears jeans and a pink hoodie. Tommy is decked out in nice blue jeans and a stylish white cotton shirt. With the top buttons open, Tommy's muscular chest is clearly visible. The couple hold hands as they walk to the car and get in. Tommy starts up the Mustang and drives the car onto Plain Road toward their romantic destination. The stars overhead are just beginning to appear as they travel the road, turning here and there, until Tommy eases the Mustang to a gentle stop on an elevated lookout where the whole valley can be seen. Tommy shuts off the engine and turns to Sarah, "Let's get out and look up at the stars." Sarah smiles with a quick nod and they both exit the car and lean against the Mustang's front end. Tommy puts his arm around Sarah and draws her close. She caves at his romantic gesture and snuggles close against Tommy. As the two sweethearts gaze up at the twinkling stars filling the night sky, Tommy glances at Sarah, "You know I love you!" Sarah lifts her face to give a tender peck and replies, "I know that, Tommy. And I love you too!" Tommy moves to stand in front. Sarah is suddenly surprised as Tommy lowers to one knee, extends his hand holding the velvet box with the Diamond Ring, and affectionately asks, "Sarah, Sweetheart - Will you marry me?" Sarah is Totally Shocked - and tears well up in her eyes as her heart races with the excitement. She tenderly looks at Tommy bend down on one knee, presenting the Diamond Ring to her - she gazes into Tommy's eyes, his face full of anticipation. Sarah clasps her fingers around Tommy's hand that holds the velvet box, and she responds with joy and glee, "Oh Tommy! Sweet Tommy! Yes! (Pause) Yes, I will marry you!" Tommy stands to his feet, removes the ring from the box, and places the Diamond on his sweetheart's finger. Sarah's eyes are big as saucers as she stares at the Diamond glittering on her finger. She turns and moves her hand every which way - admiring how the ring sparkles on her hand. Sarah gives Tommy a big long kiss - the two locked in a true moment of romantic bliss. Sarah hugs Tommy tight and remarks, "You've made me so happy! I've been waiting for this - wondering when you'd ask!" Tommy lowers his head to kiss Sarah's forehead, "That's why this military leave was so important - I wanted to "Pop the Question!" Sarah steps back and beams an infectious smile, "Carl and my parents have to the first to know." Tommy softly pokes her in the shoulder, "Grandpa already knows because I told him about it." Sarah tilts her head in a playful manner and replies, "Well, that just leaves Venture and the rest of the territory. (Giggles) I want everyone too know - I'm going to marry Tommy Long Grass!" Tommy grins and pulls Sarah in for a big hug and kiss. Then, Tommy takes Sarah's hand and suggests, "Let's give your folks the good news!" Sarah nods and they get back into the Mustang, Tommy starts the engine and heads out toward Sarah's folk's place. As Tommy drives the car to his Fiancé parent's farm, Sarah looks up at the bright stars above, then she stares at the twinkling diamond ring on her finger. She smiles a Happy Smile!

# CHAPTER TWENTY
*Honourable Discharge*

When Tommy first joined the Army which was 6 years ago, he was 21 years old. The Enlistment Form specified 4 years of Active Service, to be followed by 4 years of Reserve Service (with a provision to re-enlist another 4 years). After Tommy served the first four years, he decided to continue Active Service another 4 years. With only two years remaining on his Army Contract, Tommy at age 27, now serves as a Special Forces Senior Weapons Sergeant. He's constantly increasing his military knowledge and combat expertise. Tommy is ranked among the best in his field, and proves it year by year through annual military evaluation. Military Superiors recognize his specialized skills in selecting, training, equipping, and organizing soldiers for military service and combat. Tommy is both a military strategist and a combat warrior, a modern soldier who values Peace and is thoroughly prepared for War.

Over the next two years, Tommy's ODA unit go on different Missions, some cover a few days, others cover a few weeks. The 12-Man Team operate discretely with High-Level Clearance - guarding foreign Embassies, protecting Top Executives of Multi-National Corporations, training foreign military in the latest weaponry, and helping to eliminate dangerous radical elements. Whether in the dark of night, under the scorching sun, amid bombed-out buildings, or in the sweltering tropics - Tommy's Special Forces Unit carry out their Missions as professional soldiers - for Duty, Honour, and Country.

As his Military Enlistment draws to a close, The Army issues Tommy a Honourable Discharge in recognition of his exceptional military service. Tommy shares a unique bond with his fellow Special Forces

ODA members, they are his Battle-Buddies, and his friends-for-life. It's hard to describe the unique bond that exists when soldiers' lives depends on you, and your life depends on them. It's a military brotherhood, a friendship forged in the 'Fire' of combat, a tie that cannot be cut, severed, or destroyed by the enemy - that is what Tommy will leave with - the support, love, and respect from his Special Forces Unit. During Tommy's last evening as an enlisted soldier, Tommy is with his Army brothers for a 'Night Out' off base, at a popular Restaurant and Tavern. Everyone gathers around Tommy to share a Farewell Toast. They shower him with jokes and friendly teasing, and some share heartfelt "words-of-wisdom" for the road ahead. As the 12 soldiers stand in a loose circle, the Captain lifts his Whiskey glass and remarks, "Here's to Tommy!" Tommy scans the faces of his military brothers as they raise their glass and bellow, "To Tommy!" Everyone tilts back their glass to down the Whiskey - then, Tommy and his Unit soldiers loudly yell, "HOORAH!"

The next morning, Tommy dressed in his military uniform, holds his duffle bag as he walks to the Army Base Main Gate. As he get closer, he sees Major Strikklan, Sergeant Powers, and his unit, assembled at the Exit. The men watch as Tommy walks up to them. The group stand mere feet away from the chain link gate that people use to exit the Base. Major Strikklan looks at Tommy and remarks, "I believe I speak for all the men. (Pause) We wanted to give you one final salute!" Tommy looks at the faces of his Superior and his friends. Major Strikklan orders, "Ten-Hut!" All the soldiers snap to Attention and raise a Salute to Tommy. Major Strikklan comments, "Good Bye Senior Weapons Sergeant Tommy Long Grass! You're a Great Soldier!" Tommy stands at Attention, Salutes, "Thank You Sir! (Looks at friends) Thank You guys!" With that farewell formality over, they all shake Tommy's hand before he walks through the Gate to leave Base property. On the other side of the fence, on the civilian side, Tommy gives a final wave, then turns and walks toward the Taxi parked nearby, ready to take him to the Airport for his flight home.

# CHAPTER TWENTY-ONE
### *Return To Venture*

On the Indian Reserve, Carl pulls in his car at the Auto Shop to visit his old friend, Barry. As the master mechanic works away on a troublesome engine, Carl walks up as Barry is bent over an engine replacing some electrical wires. Barry turns his head to see Carl and remarks, "Hey buddy! What brings you here?" Carl leans in over the engine to observe his friend's handiwork, and comments, "Tommy's flying in today!" Barry stops what he's doing, straightens up to get a rag to clean his hands, then replies, "It'll be good to see him again! It seems like he's been gone forever!" Carl nods with a smile and comments, "He's been away 8 years. - Now he's coming home to stay!" Barry grins and pats Carl's shoulder, "Tell him - his old job is waiting for him when he's ready!" Carl nods his head in a pleased manner, "That's great! I'll let Tommy know when I pick him up at the Airport. (Looks around) Well, better let you get back to work, just wanted to stop by to let you to know." Barry responds, "Thanks pal!" Carl turns and walks out through the open Garage doors, and Barry grabs a screwdriver and gets back under the hood.

At the Regional Airport, the passenger jet carrying Tommy safely lands and taxis to the Terminal. The flight passengers exit and retrieve their luggage from the revolving carousels. Tommy spots his Army duffle bag and grabs the handle to pick up it. He heads toward the Terminal front entrance, exits the sliding doors and looks for his Grandpa's car. Carl sees Tommy and waves from his open car window. Tommy smiles that his Grandpa is here, and walks over to the Chevy Malibu, puts his duffle bag in the back, and gets seated and buckled up in the front. Carl looks at his grandson with a grin, "Ready to head home?" Tommy lowers his car window, chuckles and replies with in a 'Posh' tone,

"Home James!" Carl laughs at Tommy's playful quip, cranks the engine and moves out with the traffic leaving the Terminal. On route, the grandfather and grandson reminisce about the old times, and share plans about the days ahead.

Coming down the Highway and getting close, Tommy looks at the faded wood sign that announces the Indian Reservation of Venture. As Carl turns onto Reservation Road, Tommy remarks, "They should really fix up that sign!" Carl glances over and nods, "The Tribe Council voted last year to get a new sign. (Shakes head) Nothing's been done." Tommy turns his face toward Carl and comments, "If Reservation Leaders don't care - how can we expect others to care?" The grandfather nods and remarks, "Maybe you can make a difference!" Tommy stares out the window, "A difference - How?" Carl looks at his grandson and replies with confidence, "By running for a seat on Tribal Council. I believe you'd be the kind of leader our people need!" Tommy fixes his eyes on his grandfather, "You serious?" Carl glances and declares, "You bet I'm serious! We need new blood, fresh ideas, good leaders (points finger) someone like you!" Tommy leans back in the car seat, ponders a bit, then gives his answer, "Thanks Grandpa, but I can't be a politician - politicians sit around and talk - that's not me! I'm a Specialized Soldier trained for Action - not debates!" Carl looks at Tommy and accepts his grandson's candid response. As the car drives through the Reservation past familiar buildings, shops, homes, and businesses; lots of people wave as the Chevy Malibu goes by - many know Carl's car - and some recognize the young man in military uniform sitting in the front seat, and realize that Tommy has come home.

It doesn't take long for Tommy to pick up where he left off. He's back working at the Auto Shop fixing cars and trucks, much to Barry's delight. After work and on weekends, Tommy and Sarah are constantly together. The entire Reserve know the couple, and often see the two love birds - riding bikes, taking wilderness hikes, shopping stores, having romantic dinners, or casually strolling hand in hand. The young ladies in Venture, and the Hospital staff at Sarah's work, all love her Diamond engagement ring and are happy for her. Tommy puts in long hours at the Shop to earn extra money to save for the future together with Sarah. With Tommy's good income and Sarah's Nursing pay, they begin to set a date for the wedding. When there's any spare time, the excited couple go house hunting!

One day as Tommy and Sarah are driving around the area, the couple see a nice decent house and property listed "For Sale". They copy down the Real Estate Agent's phone number and call for an appointment to view the house and property. Within 48 hours, Sarah and Tommy are inside the modest house checking out the rooms and walking the grounds. The property is halfway between Sarah's folk's farm and the community of Venture, it's the perfect place for them. Both Tommy and Sarah love what they've seen and put in an offer to buy, conditional on a positive Home Inspection. The Real Estate Agent gives Tommy and Sarah the Sales Contract to sign, and Tommy gives the Agent a cheque for the Deposit. The next day, a pickup truck is parked on the property, as a Licensed Home Inspector closely examines the house from top to bottom, inside and out; the electrical wiring, the plumbing, the structural framing, all gets thoroughly inspected. After his professional work is done, the man gives Tommy and Sarah his Inspection Report - PASS - It's a good home and well made. With the favourable report, the couple close the Real Estate Sale, and soon receive the keys to their new home. As Tommy and Sarah arrive at their new property, Sarah grabs Tommy's arm with excitement and exclaims, "Oh Honey! This is ours! Imagine - Our very own house!" Tommy holds Sarah's hand in reply, "Home Sweet Home! Babe, we did it - All Ours!" The couple exit their Jeep Wrangler and walk up to the front door, insert the key and open the door. Tommy and Sarah walk inside and stand in the centre of the Living Room and gaze around at the vacant interior. Sarah points and smiles, "That's where the sofa, recliner and coffee table will go. (Pause as she turns) And over there is where we'll put the dining table and chairs." She turns to give Tommy a big hug. Tommy notices tears trickling down her cheek and asks, "Anything wrong?" Sarah looks at him with a big smile, "I'm just so happy! We're getting married (Pause) And this home is where we will raise our family (she grins) Once we have kids." Tommy throws his head back with a chuckle and squeezes Sarah in a bear hug, "Oh - we'll have kids - Lots of them!" Sarah's eyes widen and she pulls away in playful alarm, "Lots of kids?!" Tommy grins, "Yes. Lots of kids. Lots of little Tommys and Sarahs running around! (Impish grin) We can start right now!"" Sarah playfully coils back, "Oh no you don't" Tommy reaches out, "Oh yes I will!" Sarah bolts as Tommy starts to chase her around the empty rooms, both of them laughing and having fun. Tommy finally catches Sarah at the foot of the stairs and lovingly holds her. Sarah looks into Tommy eyes and softly remarks, "I surrender soldier. I'm your prisoner to do with as you please!" Tommy affectionately gazes at his sweetheart and replies, "All I want to do is Love You with all my heart for all my days!" Sarah melts at his words and she replies, "Oh Tommy! Tommy! - Kiss me!" There, at the foot of the stairs in their new home, Tommy and Sarah share a tender romantic kiss.

# CHAPTER TWENTY-TWO
## *The Rock Canyon Wedding*

The Auto Shop is busy with vehicles getting repaired when Tommy's cell phone buzzes, he looks and sees it's Sarah calling, "Hi Sweetheart!" Sarah's voice responds, "Honey, I got tomorrow off - we can go look at that spot." Tommy wipes his brow and smiles, "That's great Sweetie! I'll pick you up at O-nine hundred hours (Pause) I mean at 9 am." Sarah snickers and replies, "Sounds good Hon! See you then." Tommy chuckles at his adjustment to civilian life, "Love you babe. Bye." Sarah replies, "Love you too! Bye hon." With the call finished, Tommy pockets his cell phone and gets back to removing spark plugs on the pristine Burgundy 1963 Buick Le Sabre.

Bright and early the next morning, Tommy picks up Sarah at her place and the two head out for an area drive. Today is special and important to Sarah, today she and Tommy will look at the outdoor site where the couple want to have their Wedding Ceremony. A month earlier, Tommy traded his Jeep Wrangler in for a new Jeep Rubicon. Tommy steers the new Jeep over some local roads until he reaches the site and cuts the engine. Sarah and Tommy exit the Jeep and stand with their eyes fixed on the landscape ahead. Before them is a beautiful Rock Canyon with sculpted walls of different coloured stone. The Rock Canyon has been crafted by wind and time, and now sits as the stunning centrepiece for Sarah and Tommy's outdoor Wedding. The site has ample room for the Wedding Ceremony and attending family and guests. Sarah has a friend from High School, who works at a Florist Shop, that will help decorate the site with stunning flower arrangements. Sarah's coworker on the Nursing Team plays the Cello. The classical music will sound so lovely because of the Rock Canyon's natural acoustics. Tommy and Sarah want their Pastor to perform the

Ceremony, and Grandpa Carl will offer Prayers and Blessings in Shoshone. Sarah holds Tommy's hand as she envisions her special day. After all, everyone knows that no matter the location or the size of the venue, every Wedding is really - the Bride's Special Day!

The sky is clear, the sun is bright, and the temperature is warm and pleasant. The Wedding Day has arrived and everyone is present. Family and invited Guests, which include members of Tommy' Special Forces ODA Unit, are seated on white chairs dressed with elegant white fabric and bows. The setting is stunning with arrangements of beautiful flowers that transform the site into a breathtaking natural garden. As the Wedding Guests listen, Sarah's coworker wonderfully plays the cello filling the air with the moving music of Johann Pachelbel's "CANON in D", the stirring melody touches the heart and soul of all present. Afterwards, Grandpa Carl, dressed in a traditional Shoshone buckskin outfit decorated with ornate beadwork and silver metal disks, stands with his his arms extended over Tommy and Sarah, and chants a special Prayer and Blessing in Shoshone. When Carl is finished, he returns to his seat among the guests. As the sun shines, Sarah and Tommy stand by the Pastor with the Bridal Party nearby. A gentle breeze blows making the flower arrangements dance and sway. The scene is peaceful, lovely, and perfect. The Pastor looks over the assembled audience, gazes at Sarah and Tommy, and remarks, "Sarah and Tommy. Please look into each other's eyes to behold your Marriage Partner." Tommy and Sarah hold hands as they stare into one another's eyes. The Minister opens his thin leather Bible and reads a Scripture portion from the Gospel of John, where Jesus attended the Wedding of Canna. The Pastor talks of the Lord Jesus's Presence at that Wedding centuries ago, and it speaks of God's Presence at Sarah and Tommy's Wedding today. The Minister mentions that Jesus Blessed the Wedding Couple long ago, and the Lord Jesus still Blesses Wedding couples today. At this point, the Pastor asks Tommy and Sarah to share their Wedding Vows with each other, and to exchange the Wedding Rings. At the giving and receiving of wedding rings on the couple's hand, the Pastor smiles, looks at the couple and comments, "I now pronounce you Husband and Wife! (To Tommy) You may kiss your Bride!" The Minister scarcely has the words out when Tommy and Sarah lock onto each other with a powerful kiss! All the Family and Guests erupt with loud Cheers and Applause. The Canyon walls reverberate with joyous noise and celebration! On cue, someone releases a flock of white doves that soar in the sky above, circling in the air, then fly away.

Later at the Wedding Reception, there's festive decorations, and a DJ plays popular tunes and requests. Lovely floral arrangements decorate each table, and Family and Guests have a meal choice between - roast Chicken, brazed beef, or grilled salmon; complimented by glazed baby potatoes, steamed fresh vegetables, and choice of Salads - Garden, Caesar, or Coleslaw. Fresh bread sticks and ample butter trays are available for all. After the meal is finished, those at the Reception have opportunity to enjoy Cherries Jubilee, S'mores Donuts, tiny Strawberry cupcakes, and Apple Pie Butter Tarts. All the guests and relatives are having a great time, enjoying the food, loving the desserts, sharing speeches, and drinking toasts. The atmosphere in the room is festive, fun, and fabulous! Sarah and Tommy cut the eye-popping Wedding Cake amid a flurry of photos taken by family and friends. The Bride and Groom visit each table delivering the Wedding Cake sample and to personally Thank each person for their attendance. When Sarah and Tommy reach the table where Tommy's Army buddies are seated, all the soldiers stand at Attention and Salute the Bride and Groom with a boisterous "HOORAH!" Tommy introduces Sarah to each of his former ODA Unit members, who are proud and delighted to meet Tommy's beautiful Bride. The new couple continue to circulate through the Room greeting and Thanking guests, when they finish, Sarah tugs on Tommy's arm, smiles and comments, "Time for our Dance!" Tommy smiles and gets the DJ's attention and signals.

At that moment, the room's lighting changes from bright dining illuminance to a romantic ambiance. Everyone watches as the Bride and Groom move to position in the middle of the dance floor. With soft colourful lights as a background, and their favourite song playing, Sarah and Tommy share their very first dance as Husband and Wife. There, alone on the dance floor, Sarah and Tommy move and sway to the sweet melody of their romantic song. When the song finishes and the couple stop, everyone cheers and heartily applauds. Then, the DJ begins to play lively catchy tunes that has everyone moving and grooving. Some of the Couple's younger relatives are out on the floor 'Busting Moves' with youthful energy. As the music plays, the people, young and old, dance and have a great time celebrating Sarah and Tommy getting married. The entire day, from the Rock Canyon

Wedding, the delicious Reception Dinner, to the Dance Party - it all makes for a truly remarkable event. An outstanding day for everyone!

# CHAPTER TWENTY-THREE
*Little Home Sweet Home*

As newly weds, Tommy and Sarah are excited to set up their first-ever home together. Some guys from the Auto Shop and local friends from the Reservation lend muscle to bring in the newly bought furniture: dressers, beds, tables, cabinets, chairs, and a big sofa. Sarah has some friends and hospital coworkers lend a hand to arrange and organize the kitchen, and set up the master bedroom and the two spare bedrooms. To anyone watching, it's a beehive of activity, as guys and gals go in and out of the front and back door, bringing in household items from the moving truck parked in the driveway. With all the help, it doesn't take long for the house to have items and furniture in all the rooms, from the upstairs to the main floor. Tommy and Sarah check on the moving truck and see that it sits empty - everything has been moved in. They walk through the open front door and take a look inside - all the guys and gals are sitting or standing around talking, catching their breath, or just plain resting, A few look hot, sweaty and tired. Sarah pulls out her cell phone, taps the screen and pockets the phone. As she holds Tommy's hand, the newly weds smile as they look at the faces their friends. Sarah cheerfully announces, "Thanks to everyone for helping us move in! (Arm around Tommy) We couldn't have done it without you." Tommy chimes in, "Thanks to everyone! Really - we appreciate it!" Sarah adds, "we know you guys must be hungry - so we've got my mom, dad, and Grandpa Carl, bringing us a 'ton of food'!" The entire group give out a big cheer, "YAY!" Just as Sarah finishes speaking - vehicle horns sound in the driveway, "HONK! HONK!" Tommy and Sarah peek out the front entrance to see Sarah's dad and mom arrive in their big pickup truck with Carl's Malibu right behind. Tommy, Sarah, and a few friends close by, go to greet and help cart food inside. Sarah's dad lifts the truck's cargo cover, and Carl pops the Malibu trunk, to reveal big plastic containers filled with all kinds of food. Sarah's parents and Carl brought lots to eat - there's pizza slices, pasta, fried chicken, corn dogs, hamburgers, hot dogs, potato and macaroni salads, cans of beer, soda pop, refreshing coolers, and a bunch of snack food. As the young people stand by, Carl and Sarah's parents start off-loading food containers to them, which they happily carry into the house. Soon, the dining room table, the kitchen table and counters are loaded with a variety of food. Although everyone is famished and ready to eat, they politely wait for Sarah and Tommy to join them. As the people gather in clusters around the food, Tommy whistles to get everyone's attention, "Before we eat and 'Chow Down' (looks at Carl) I'd like my Grandpa Carl to pray the Blessing." As Carl takes a step forward, everyone bows their head and closes their eyes. Carl bows with his eyes closed and prays, "Dear Heavenly Father, Thank you for these young people who have helped Tommy and Sarah to move into their new home! Thank you for all this wonderful food! We give Thanks to You and ask for Your Blessing. Amen!" As Carl finishes, the young men and women quickly begin to load up their paper plates with all kinds of edibles. People are happily talking, conversing, and politely minding one another as food items are being selected and picked up. In a matter of minutes, the couple's new home is filled with people sitting, standing, crouched down, or parked on the floor, busy eating and enjoying their food. With healthy fit young people, there's always room for 'Seconds', and for a few 'Thirds'. As the sounds of happy people and friendly conversation fills their new home, Sarah and Tommy gaze around at their friends, Sarah's parents, and Carl. Sarah squeezes Tommy's arm and softly remarks, "I want our home to be a happy place! A place where people can feel love and respect." Tommy kisses Sarah's forehead, "It will be, Hon! We'll make sure it does!" The newly weds bask in the warm atmosphere, surrounded by loving family and good friends.

Six months later…

Tommy and Sarah's home is an oasis and relaxing refuge from the busy world. Inspiring pictures and sweet family photos line the walls, and Sarah decorates the house with fresh flowers. Anyone visiting would find a happy home where there's peace, joy and love. The couple change one of the spare rooms to someday be a baby's room. Tommy and Sarah prep and paint the walls in a soft pastel colour,

Tommy assembles a new baby crib, and Sarah puts up nice curtains. When they are finished, the future baby room looks loving and precious. As they step back to take in their handiwork, Sarah and Tommy look at the empty baby crib. Tommy gazes at Sarah with a tender smile, "All we need now is a baby!" Sarah playfully replies, "Hey! I can't do it alone. (pokes Tommy) Remember, it takes two!" Tommy chuckles and gives Sarah a hug.

# CHAPTER TWENTY-FOUR
*The Agency Comes Calling*

On the outside, Tommy and Sarah's house looks warm and nice with flower beds and manicured shrubs out front. A beautiful wreath decorates the front door. Field birds merrily chirp from the trees and grassy meadow nearby. The setting is pretty as a postcard. Inside the home, there's the tantalizing aroma of fresh baked bread, the soothing scent of lavender plants, and the warmth of family photos and endearing knick-knacks. Inside and outside, the house is a wonderful place!

Tommy and Sarah are relaxing on the sofa when they hear the crush of heavy tires on the gravel driveway. They look through the front window to see two big black SUVs with dark tinted windows roll onto the property. Tommy and Sarah watch as the doors of the first SUV open. Three big men wearing dark sunglasses, dressed in white shirts, black suits and ties, exit and stand on the ground. The men begin to walk toward the house. Tommy and Sarah go to the front entrance, open the door and stand on the front porch. The couple watch as the three big strangers approach and stand in front. Tommy's military training kicks in, he notices the 'Out-of-State' plates, and steps in front of Sarah to protect her. He cautiously asks, "Good Day gentleman! May I ask why you're on our land? Do you need directions?" The man in the centre with blonde hair replies, "Thank you for your offer to assist, but I don't think we're lost. We're looking for Senior Weapons Sergeant Tommy Long Grass! Do we have the right address?" Tommy and Sarah exchange glances, and Tommy replies, "I'm Tommy Long Grass. Why are you looking for me?" The lead man injects, "The Tommy Long Grass who helped to rescue a female NGO in Afghanistan!" Tommy is surprised, since only his ODA Team and

Military Superiors were privy to such knowledge. The man anticipates Tommy's upcoming question and continues, "My name is Agent Brooks! We're part of a Secret Government Agency. (Pause) May we speak with you?" By now, Tommy is relaxed and turns to Sarah to ask, "Is it okay if we go inside to talk?" Sarah glances at the men and softly replies, "Sure Hon. If you think it's okay." Tommy looks at the three Agents and confidently remarks, "I think it'll be okay Sweetie." Tommy turns toward the three visitors and extends his arm toward the open door, "Gentlemen, please come inside so we can talk." Sarah turns to go inside, and Tommy and the men follow. As Tommy invites the men to be seated on the sofa and chairs, Sarah is in the kitchen getting refreshments for the visitors. She asks from the confines of the kitchen, "Will you men like any coffee, tea, or beverage?" Agent Brooks responds, "Thank you Ma'am! That would be very nice - coffee and beverages would be fine." Soon, Sarah brings a tray with mugs of hot coffee and bottles of soda pop, and sets it down on the coffee table. In a couple minutes, she returns with a platter of cookies, biscuits, salami rolls, cheese squares, and small plates. As Sarah sits beside Tommy, he eyes the refreshments and comments, "Looks good darling. Thank you!" Tommy coaxes the three men, "Go ahead, please." The lead Agent and his two associates politely grab a coffee mug and put some snacks on their plates. After Agent Brooks takes a sip of coffee, he sets down his mug and looks directly into Tommy's eyes, "We, the Agency, have intel that a Drug Cartel is making a new drug in the Amazon Rainforest." At this point, the Agent pulls out a paper and unfolds a Map of the Amazon Rainforest. All eyes are on the Map as the man continues, "The drug is highly addictive and lethal, just a tiny amount will kill. (Sips coffee) We know they're in this area. (finger on Map) Our Agents haven't been able to locate the Cartel. That's why we need you with your Special Forces Recon skills." Tommy focuses on the Map, then glances at Sarah and replies, "I'm no longer in Active Service, just a civilian living peacefully at home. (Pause) What about other Special Ops?" The Agent shifts his position and leans forward, "As important as this Mission is - The Government is focused overseas on big international problems affecting our Allies. Our Agency has been tapped to deal with this threat!… Tommy, we would not be here asking for your help if there was another way. As it stands - there isn't! In a matter of weeks, if not sooner, reliable sources tell us the Drug Cartel will unleash this deadly drug across America - Thousands, perhaps millions of American lives will be lost. We can't let that happen! - Will you help? Help us find this Cartel and give us the GPS coordinates? We'll send in our drones to do the rest!" Tommy leans back as he holds his wife's hand, he thinking real hard. Tommy's strong sense of Military Service regarding duty, honour, and country, floods his soul. Sarah sees his inner struggle. She turns to Tommy and comments, "I want you here, but if you need to go - I understand." Tommy looks at Sarah, then glances at the three Agents. He remarks, "You said thousands, perhaps millions of lives will die if this new drug hits our country?" The lead Agent replies, "Yes Sir! This drug is so toxic and lethal - only a small drop will kill you!" Tommy stands up with resolve, "Only one thing to do - Find this Drug Cartel and wipe them out!" Agent Brooks remarks, "Tomorrow, I'll give you the Mission details". At this point, the three Agents rise to their feet, and Agent Brooks expresses his appreciation, "Thank you Sergeant Long Grass! Your country still needs you! The Map can stay - you'll need it!" Sarah stands to hug Tommy to support. Tommy gazes down at his sweetheart and asks aloud, "How long will the Mission be?" The main Agent responds, "A few days, or a few weeks - whatever it takes! - These criminals are very elusive." Tommy looks into the leader's eyes and remarks, "I'll do this only on one condition." The Agent replies, "What's the condition?" Tommy gazes down at Sarah, then looks at the agents, "I want to assemble my own Recon Team." At those words, the three agents nod and begin to leave when Tommy interjects, "For the Recon Team - I want Ninjans on it!" The three agents turn about puzzled by Tommy's comment, and Brooks asks, "What are Ninjans?" Tommy grins and firmly responds, "Ninjans are American Indians highly skilled in Martial Arts! Ninjans are even more secretive that your secret Agency!" The three agents look at each other, then step aside for a quiet huddle. When they finish, Agent Brooks approaches Tommy and comments, "Affirmative! Form your Recon Team - Ninjans included!" After the Agents exit the house, Tommy and Sarah walk to the front door and watch the three men climb back into the their SUV. The engines start, and the two black SUVs back out of the driveway and onto the road, and soon disappear from sight. Sarah looks at Tommy and hugs him, "Honey, I'm so proud of you!" Tommy wonders for a second about the choice and asks, "You sure it's okay?" Sarah gives a firm stare and replies, "Imagine if someone we knew got killed by that drug! Tommy, Do it for all of us! (Pause) Do it for our future children!" As Sarah leaves to clean up, Tommy closes the front door with a determined expression.

# CHAPTER TWENTY-FIVE
## *Creating Ninjan Recon*

Sarah has gone to bed for the evening, and Tommy sits at the kitchen table with the Map of the Amazon spread out in front of him. His eyes go to and fro as he studies the Map's topography and geography details. He soon realizes how massive and far-reaching the Amazon Rainforest truly is. The Rainforest not only covers Brazil, but it crosses national boundaries and extends into other countries like Venezuela, Columbia, Peru, and Bolivia. The Amazon is unlike any other place in the world, so beautiful, yet so deadly! The Amazon is beautiful with its numerous rivers, countless tributaries, tropical trees, dense jungle, exotic flowers, and scenic wonder; but it's also very deadly due to the poisonous plants, snakes, insects, wild animals, and the infamous flesh-eating Piranha. This is the terrain where Tommy must hunt for the elusive Drug Cartel. As he studies the map, he realizes it will be like looking for a 'needle-in-a-haystack'. There's so much territory and such formidable surroundings. The quickest and easiest way to travel is by boat on the river systems. The most challenging is to travel by land - hacking your way through the jungle and dense brush, cutting a path over ground, where perhaps, no civilized human has gone before. Tommy folds up the Map and calls it a night. He goes upstairs, freshens up, then climbs in bed beside Sarah, gives her a Good Night kiss, adjusts his pillow and drifts off to sleep.

Early the next morning, As Sarah and Tommy are having Breakfast, there is a KNOCK on the front door. Tommy goes to open the door to find Agent Brooks standing on the porch, holding a thick military folder. Tommy invites the man inside, "Please come in, we're having Breakfast. - Want some?" Brooks smiles and replies, Thanks Sergeant, but we had Breakfast in town earlier." As they walk toward the kitchen, Tommy asks, "Where are the other two?" Brooks responds, "They're waiting in the SUV." Tommy understands and points to an empty chair, "Agent Brooks, please sit down." The man gets seated and places the thick folder on the table beside him. Sarah brings over a clean mug and pours Brooks a fresh coffee and enquires, "You can join us - there's plenty of food!" The Agent politely smiles and comments, "Thank you Mrs. Long Grass, the coffee will be just fine!" Sarah returns to the Kitchen counter where she is cleaning and cutting vegetables for the evening dinner. As Agent Brooks sips his coffee, Tommy eyes the folder and remarks, "Mission details in that?" Agent Brooks, sets aside his mug and opens the folder to bring out Papers and Intel Reports. During his time with the Special Forces, Tommy recalls such folders when getting briefed on Missions. Brooks sifts through the papers and lays out three Reports before Tommy. The Agent remarks, "These Reports contain the latest Intel on how the Cartel operates, and where they're most likely be in the Rainforest. For your 6-Man Recon Team, the Agency has assigned two Ex-Special Forces operatives." Tommy nods and picks up a Report and peruses it, "I'll give you a list of the weapons, equipment, and supplies we will need." The Agent gives a nod as he drinks his coffee. Tommy lifts up another Report and glances through it, then sets it down, "How will the Recon Team get to the Amazon?" Brooks looks at Tommy and replies, "When the Team is assembled - Everyone will rendezvous at an 'undisclosed Airstrip', where a plane will fly you to Columbia. From there, you will take a small plane across the border into Brazil." Tommy studies the Papers and comments, "We'll need a good chopper - the Bell 407 is small enough to fly the jungle, and big enough to carry our supplies." Agent Brooks confirms, "You'll have your Bell 407 helicopter!" Tommy smiles, "Good!" As Tommy slides his empty Breakfast plate to the side, he asks, "Agent Brooks, tell me more about the Mission and the Drug Cartel we're up against." With the background of Sarah humming melodies as she washes and cuts vegetables at the kitchen sink, Agent Brooks begins to share more vital Intel and details regarding to the Mission. At one point, Brooks comments, "This Mission needs a name!" Tommy thinks for a second and confidently replies, "OPERATION TOMAHAWK". Agent Brooks ponders as he quietly repeatedly the words to himself, then asks "Why Operation Tomahawk?" Tommy looks at Brooks and replies, "The Tomahawk was always a key weapon for American Indians. Since the Recon Team will have Ex-Special Forces and Ninjans. The name is fitting - besides, Operation Tomahawk is catchy and sounds deadly!" Brooks smiles, "Operation Tomahawk. Copy that!"  For the rest of that morning, Tommy and Agent Brooks talk about the drug threat and critical aspects of the Mission. After the Agent has thoroughly briefed Tommy, the two leave the kitchen, and Tommy walks Agent Brooks to the SUV. Brooks gets seated and rolls down his window, "Please tell your wife Thanks for the coffee! (signals pull out, then looks at Tommy) Have a Good Day Sergeant Long Grass. - We'll be in touch." At that, the big black SUV leaves the property. Tommy returns inside and walks over to help his new bride at the counter. He stands next to Sarah and she asks, "Get all the information you need?" Tommy gives her a sweet peck on top of her hair and replies, "Everything is fine! Got all the Intel and Coordinates for the job. Sarah smiles as she cleans some lettuce. Tommy continues, "Now, I have to set up a meeting with the Ninjans!" Tommy goes to sit at the kitchen table and pulls out his cell phone and dials. Grandpa Carl answers on the third ring, "Hi Tommy! How are things?" Tommy responds, "Sarah and I are doing fine. - Grandpa, there's something very important I need to speak with the Ninjans about. Can you help set up a meeting right away - say late tonight, or tomorrow some time?" Carl is silent for a few seconds, then the man replies, "Sure Tommy! kind of sudden - but is must be really important, or you wouldn't have asked." Tommy appreciates his Grandfather's help, "Thanks Grandpa! It's extremely important - that's the reason for the meeting." Carl closes the conversation, "Ok Tommy! I'll call you back when things are set up." With the phone call finished, Tommy picks up the folder packed with Papers, Reports, and the Amazon Map, and carries it to the coffee table and lays it down. He grabs a pen and large notepad, sits on the sofa and stares at the folder - the wheels in his head are turning, Mission plans and strategy are formulating. Tommy takes a breath and begins to write down action plans. After lots of notes and scribbled diagrams, somewhere close to 5 pm, Carl calls and Tommy answers, "Hi Grandpa! What did they say?" Carl's voice comes over the phone speaker loud and clear, "The meeting is set for 3 pm tomorrow at Eli Waters' Horse Ranch - Canyon Run." Tommy is thrilled and replies, "Great news Grandpa! I'll see you there. Bye!" Tommy sits back on the sofa and breathes a sigh of relief. Meeting with the Ninjans is only the half of it - he still has to persuade them to join a dangerous covert Mission - in a distant country - on a Continent far away!"

* * *

The next day, Tommy drives his Jeep Rubicon out to the Canyon Run Ranch. He spots vehicles parked outside the big Arena Barn, and recognizes Grandpa Carl's Malibu. Tommy parks alongside the other cars, and he exits and goes inside the Barn. As he opens the Barn's sliding door, Tommy sees Carl and a group of men standing in the middle of the Arena dirt floor. Tommy strides over with a smile and greets everyone, "Hi everybody! Thanks for meeting with me on such short notice!" Tommy hasn't seen some of these men for over 8 years, he makes eye contact with each man. There's Morgan Jeffrey, his old Sensi from the Gold Eagle Dojo, Barry Armstrong, his current boss at the Auto Shop, Steve Osprey, a local welder and metal fabricator, Eli Waters, owner of the Canyon Run Horse Ranch, and lastly, his Grandfather, Carl Long Grass.

As the men look at Tommy, Eli asks, "Tommy, your Grandpa said this meeting is very important. - What's it about?" Tommy glances at the faces of the men before him, and replies, "As everyone here knows, I've just finished Military Service, married Sarah, and we've began to set up our home. To my surprise, a Secret Government Agency contacted me about a vital Mission - Stop a Drug Cartel making a new deadly drug in the Amazon Rainforest. (Makes eye contact) This new drug is dangerous and lethal - only a small drop will kill anyone. (Pause) Unless stopped, this Drug Cartel will soon unleash this deadly drug across America - thousands, maybe millions will die!" All the men are shocked at the news. Steve Osprey remarks, "How does this involve us?" Tommy steps forward and looks at everyone, "The Agency has tasked me to form a Recon Unit to go against the Cartel - I need three Ninjans to join! - It'll be challenging, dangerous, and perhaps deadly! - No matter what - the Drug Cartel MUST BE STOPPED! This drug CANNOT REACH AMERICA!" The men are visibly moved at hearing of such a threat, and Morgan speaks up, "What role do we play in this?" Tommy gazes at his old Sensi and remarks, "I'm not asking you to be Army Special Forces Soldiers, two others and myself will handle that part. - But I will need Ninjans for their Stealth, Camouflage, Weaponry, and Ninja Skills." Tommy stops speaking and watches as the men move aside to talk among themselves. Grandpa Carl walks over to his grandson and puts his arm on Tommy's shoulder, "Give them a few minutes, Tommy. What you're asking of them is big! There are some hard decisions to be made." As the men break from their huddle, they look over at the grandson and grandfather. Morgan, Eli and Steve, walk over to Tommy and stand resolute before the young man. Morgan firmly remarks, "Tommy, we will join your Recon Mission! We've decided to do our part - this dangerous drug must not enter the United States!" Tommy smiles and shakes each man's hand to express his gratitude. As the men regroup in a loose circle on the arena floor, Tommy announces, "We meet at my house early tomorrow morning to go over plans and details. Be sure to bring all your Ninjan supplies and weapons.(the men acknowledge) (Tommy pauses and grins) We're calling the Mission - OPERATION TOMAHAWK!" Hearing the Mission's name, Carl and the fellow Ninjans break into big smiles, and Eli lifts up his head and lets loose a loud Shoshone **WAR CRY!**

The following day, bright and early, the pickup truck carrying Morgan, Steve and Eli, pull onto Tommy and Sarah's property. The three Ninjans exit the truck and get their Ninjan weapons and gear out of the cargo box. Tommy heard the truck arrive and opens the front door and waves the trio to come inside. The three men carry their gear and weapons, and enter the house. Tommy closes the door. Once inside, Morgan asks, "Where do we put our stuff?" Tommy points to a back room off the kitchen and replies, "Mission gear and weapons go in the back room." The men cart their stuff into the room and set their belongings together in a pile, they rejoin Tommy in the Kitchen. Sarah has just made fresh coffee, bacon and eggs, hash browns, and buttered toast. The aroma of breakfast is too much for Steve and he remarks, "That sure smells good!" Sarah smiles and offers, "Pull up a kitchen chair and dig in. I made it for you guys!" Eli, Steve, and Morgan, pull out chairs at the table and eagerly wait, as Sarah brings mugs of coffee, glasses of orange juice, and plates with freshly scrambled eggs, bacon, hash browns, and buttered toast. The guys dig into the morning breakfast, enjoying the food and couple's company. As they are talking, there's a KNOCK on the front door. Tommy gets up and comments, "It must be Agent Brooks!" Tommy goes to open the front door and invites the Government Agent inside. As the two enter the kitchen area, Tommy makes the introductions, "Guys - this is Agent Brooks, Code Name 'Poppa Bear', our Handler for the Mission. (Points) This is Eli Waters, Steve Osprey, and Morgan Jeffrey - our Ninjans on the Team." Agent Brooks nods a greeting and sits down in the chair Tommy has pulled out for him. With everyone around the kitchen table, Agent Brooks retrieves a folded note from his dark blazer, and comments as he hands it to Tommy, "Here is the location where you fly out from. Our two Ex-Special Forces soldiers will join up there. The Gulfstream will take 6-7 hours to reach Columbia, South America. When the Recon Team lands, you transfer to a small cargo plane to fly you from Columbia to a secret airstrip in the Amazon Jungle. Your Bell 407 chopper will be waiting for you there." Tommy unfolds the paper and checks the info, then nods to Brooks. Tommy hands two folder paper sheets to Brooks and comments, "Here's the list of military weapons, tactical gear, and supplies for the Mission." Agent Brooks tucks the papers inside his blazer, "I'll see your Team gets everything you need!" When Tommy and Brooks finish, Sarah asks the Agent, "Would you like some coffee and breakfast?" Brooks smiles and replies, "Yes Ma'am! I'm feeling hungry this morning!" Within a minute, Sarah brings Agent Brooks a mug of fresh-brewed coffee, and a hearty breakfast plate. The kitchen has become a folksy scene, as everyone sits at the table having their breakfast and sharing conversation like old friends.

When everyone has eaten their fill, and sit quietly at the table, Agent Brooks stands up and looks at the group, "I want to Thank You men for joining this important Mission! Your skills make all the difference - it will help us 'Win The Day'! Good Luck and God Speed!" Tommy stands to see Brooks to the front door. As the Agent opens the door to leave, Tommy enquires, "Mission communication secured?" Brooks stops in the doorway and nods, "Affirmative Sergeant! The Coms are set for Operation Tomahawk! Your equipment is already on the jet." Tommy replies with a firm grin as Brooks exits the house, "Copy That Poppa Bear!" Tommy watches as Agent Brooks enters the Black SUV and it drives off the property and down the road out of sight. The sounds of spirited conversation makes Tommy turn his head toward the kitchen. He closes the front door, and hears laughter coming from the room. When Tommy enters the kitchen, he sees everyone snickering and Sarah giggling. Tommy remarks, "Hey guys - what did I miss?" They look at Tommy and keep laughing. He looks and Sarah is almost crying she's laughing so hard. Tommy is exasperated and demands, "Come on - let me in on it!" Sarah tries to talk, but breaks out laughing, then she tries again, "We all laughing at Eli's comment!" Tommy looks at Eli and the man tilts his head and shrugs his shoulders. Tommy again asks, "Well - what was it?" Sarah regains her composure and replies, "We were talking about getting things done -

and Eli said he likes doing stuff at the top of the hour …like 1 o'clock, 2 o'clock…   Eli said if things start on the half-hour (Sarah snickers) things only get 'Half Done'!" Morgan laughs as he points at Eli, "Don't want things 'Half-Baked do we?!" Steve can't resist ribbing his friend, "Do you get 25 cents every 'quarter' hour?" Eli throws his hands in the air, "You guys - Stop it!" Tommy begins to chuckle. Eli looks at Tommy and quips, "Not you too!" As everyone starts to settle down again, Sarah comments, "Who wants more coffee?" The men raise their hands, and Morgan comments, "Sarah. You make really good coffee!" As Sarah brews a fresh pot of coffee, Tommy and the Ninjans continue their friendly time around the kitchen table.

# CHAPTER TWENTY-SIX
*The Hunt Begins*

Two vehicles roll along a remote County road in the dead of night, they travel past sleepy farms and ranches, and go over wilderness areas. Tommy and Morgan are in the Jeep Rubicon in the lead, and Eli and Steve ride in the pickup truck behind. The headlights of the Jeep catch the reflective road sign up ahead - Fletcher Air Field and Flight School. Tommy slows down and turns left to take the gravel road toward a set of Aluminum buildings that sit shrouded in the dark. The pick up truck follows right behind. Rolling up near the main building, Tommy presses the driver window down, sticks his head out and peers about. Suddenly, he sees headlights 'Flash On-Off' some distance away. Tommy moves the gearshift and drives across the grassy fields toward the flashing headlights. Eli and Steve follow. As Tommy gets near, the Jeep headlights illuminate the two black SUVs parked near the Air Field Runway. A 12-passenger Gulfstream Jet painted dark grey sits parked on the nearby airstrip. When the Jeep gets close, Agent Brooks and his two Associates exit and stand beside the first SUV. Tommy stops the Jeep, parks and turns off the engine. Eli pulls up beside the Jeep and he cuts the truck engine. Tommy and the Ninjans get out of their vehicles, grab their big black duffle bags filled with weapons, gear, and supplies. They begin walking toward the SUVs. There, out in the middle of no-where, at an obscure rural airfield, 2 am in the morning, pitch black all around, Tommy and the three Ninjans are secretly meeting with Agent Brooks and his two associates.

As the four men approach, Agent Brooks lifts his arm and circles his hand - immediately, the jet engines of the Gulf Stream start to whirl, and the plane's exterior and interior lights turn on. A crewman opens the side passenger door and access steps drop down. Agent Brooks looks at Tommy and remarks, "Glad you made it!" Tommy replies, "You sure picked a real backwoods airstrip!" Brooks grins and comments, "In our line of work - the more remote the better!" By now, the jet engines have a high-pitched whine, the engine turbines turning fast. At that moment, Brooks waves a signal and the passenger doors of the second SUV open. Two big men fully dressed in black tactical combat uniforms, carrying large black military duffle bags, exit the SUV and approach to stand beside Agent Brooks. Tommy gives the duo a quick study, and Brooks comments, "These are the two Ex-Special Forces soldiers the Agency is sending with your Team." The lead Agent gestures, "On my left is Tasker. (Motions) On my right is Roberts. (Pause) Two of our best operatives! I gave them the same Map I gave you." Tommy remarks, "Copy  That!", then he steps forward to greet and shake each man's hand, "Tasker. Roberts. Welcome to Operation Tomahawk! Thank you for joining us!" Tasker and Roberts reply with a hearty handshake and an affirmative nod. Agent Brooks remarks, "Sergeant Long Grass has Lead on this Op - He's in Charge. Understood!" Tasker and Roberts firmly respond, "Copy that, Sir!" With the introduction formality over, Brooks comments, "The plane is ready. (Looks at Tommy) Go find us a Drug Cartel!" Tommy loudly responds, "HOORAH!" He and the Recon Team move toward the jet, quickly climb the access steps and enter the plane. Through the oval side windows, Agent Brooks observes the Team members pick out their cabin chair and get seated for the flight. A crewman shuts and secures the side door, and the plane's two jet engines produce a high-pitched whine. As the jet begins to move, Tommy looks out at Brooks standing in front of the SUV, and gives the Agent a 'parting wave'. In a matter of seconds, the jet zooms forward and quickly reaches Take Off - the plane ascends at a steep angle, and soon flies high above the clouds blanketing the nighttime sky. The plane's interior lights are dimmed making the passenger cabin quiet and cosy. Tommy sits back in the comfortable leather cabin chair and glances around at the Team. Everyone appears settled in for the flight - a flight that will carry them over the United States, across Mexico and Latin America, to finally land in Columbia, South America. Tommy relines his cabin chair to relax and close his eyes. The interior is quiet and peaceful, there's only the faint sound of rushing air heard through the plane's windows, as the jet flies at 40,000 feet above sea level.

The morning sun has risen in the sky, it's 9 am Columbia time when the Gulfstream sets down at a South American Airport. Agent Brooks has arranged Official Clearance for a Short C-23 Sherpa cargo plane to be fuelled and ready for departure to Brazil. Tommy and the Recon Team transfer their gear up the cargo ramp into the plane interior. Everyone gets strapped in. With all the Team and Mission gear onboard, Tommy gives the pilot the signal to leave. The aircraft's two big metal propellors rev up and the plane begins to taxi to the runway, and waits on the tarmac for Control Tower Clearance. With the okay from Air Traffic Control, the Short C-23 cargo plane moves down the runway picking up speed as the big propellors roar. Inside the plane, everyone feels the bumps and gets jostled as the plane's tires go faster and faster over the runway tarmac. Reaching top speed, the Cargo plane Takes Off from the Columbian Airport, and climbs higher and higher, until it reaches cruising height, heading in a South-East direction toward Brazil. As the planes flies sure and steady, Tommy calls for a group huddle around the unfolded Map of the Amazon Rainforest. All Team members gather around and Tommy conveys Mission objective, strategy, and details. Inside the cargo plane, the ride is a bit bumpy as the pilots encounter air turbulence. Tommy points to a location marked with a red X, and explains that is the Jungle Airstrip where a Bell 407 Helicopter waits for them. Tommy glances at the faces of his Team and remarks, "Any Questions?" One of the Ex-Special Forces soldiers asks, "Where's the Drug Cartel operating?" Tommy points and circles his hand over a portion of the Map, and replies, "The Cartel have been seen here." The soldier nods. Tommy glances at the Team and continues, "They could be here (points) or elsewhere (hand sweeps across map). If needed, we'll use the Chopper to cover a wider area - Look for signs of any movement, labs, or camps." As the Team quietly confer, Tommy folds up the Map. He sits back in his cargo hold seat and refastens his harness. The others go back to their seats and get strapped in.

From Agent Brooks' intel, the flight from Columbia to Brazil will be a little over 3 hours. Tommy scans his wristwatch - it reads 9:30 am on the face. The young man whistles to get everyone's attention, then shouts loud to be heard above the noisy propellers, "We reach the jungle airstrip in 2.5 hours. Time to Check and Prep our Mission gear!" The Team members acknowledge and everyone brings out their weapons, gear, and supplies, to inspect and double-check items.

Tommy pulls over his big black military duffle bag, and brings out his **M4A1 carbine** and ammo rounds for close inspection. Throughout the plane's cargo interior, Team members are examining their weapons and gear. Tasker opens his black duffle bag and brings out his Heckler & Koch **HK416 assault rifle**. Beside him, Roberts unzips his duffle bag and brings out his **FN SCAR battle rifle** and ammo clips. Eli Waters pulls out his **black Ninjan bow** and black leather sheaths full of deadly **black arrows**. Steve Armstrong gets his weapon - the ninjan long **black chain dart** and sharp **Shuriken** throwing stars. Morgan Jeffrey opens his bag to retrieve his fierce **eagle claw battle batons** and his Ninjan swords - the short **Ninjato** and the long **Katana** sword. Tommy looks at the Recon Team as they check their gear and have weapons ready. Tommy is pleased at the Team's preparedness. He glances at his watch - soon they will be in Brazil - scouting the Amazon Rainforest for the elusive Drug Cartel.

Two hours later, the cargo plane enters the air space to cross the border into Brazil. The Short C-23 prop plane drops to a lower altitude and flies above the jungle tree line. Tommy and Team peer out the cargo hold windows to see the dense foliage of tree tops that resembles a sea of green as far as the eye can see. After a number of minutes, the pilots circle the plane above an open clearing created in the dense Jungle. The crude jungle airstrip is nothing more than an uneven dirt runway that's been hastily prepared. Off to the side in another clearing sits the Bell 407 helicopter. The Pilots circle again and start the descent to land. Tommy and the others watch out the windows as the plane dips below the tree tops and comes to land on the dirt runway. The Short C-23 Sherpa Cargo plane was engineered and designed for short Take Offs and Landings on unpaved runways. It's the perfect aircraft for the jungle airstrip. The plane safely lands and rolls on the dirt airstrip until the engines cut and the propellors stop. The Recon Team exit the plane and Tommy waves gratitude to the two C-23 Sherpa pilots. As the Team gathers beside the airstrip, the cargo plane turns around to position on the runway. The Pilots throttle the big engines making the propellors roar, and the plane zooms forward and Takes Off from the remote runway. Tommy and Team watch as the Short C-23 Sherpa cargo plane flies away. Standing beside the crude airstrip, the Recon Team quickly move toward the helicopter. As they approach, the chopper pilot steps out to greet Tommy and Team. Tommy remarks, "You our Mission Pilot?" The man wearing the baseball cap, aviation

Sunglasses, with scruffy beard, nods and replies, "The name is Cortez. Juan Cortez. Agent Brooks briefed me about your Team. The Mission equipment you requested is inside." Tommy and the Chopper Pilot shake hands, then Tommy remarks, "Time to Rock n Roll!" He motions the Team to load the equipment and supplies inside the Chopper. As the Team get in, Tommy takes the passenger seat beside the chopper pilot. The helicopter confines become tight as the Team and bulky bags of Mission gear cram the limited space. Team members have to adjust positions to accommodate each another, Tasker grins and jests, "This makes for nice and cosy!" Steve comments, "Hope no one wants to change seats, (chuckles) It just won't happen!" At that remark, everyone laughs and settles in for the ride to Base Camp - a circled GPS location on the Amazon Rainforest Map secured in Tommy's combat vest.

# CHAPTER TWENTY-SEVEN
## *Jungle Tactics*

The Chopper flies straight to the GPS coordinates on the Map. The Pilot, Cortez, has lots of experience flying the Amazon Jungle. He is a "Chopper For Hire" and fluent in Portuguese. He has ferried all sorts of passengers - gold miners, loggers, Botanists, tourists, and even Missionaries. This is the man's first time carrying an Ex-Military Recon Team packing heavy firepower. Agent Brooks met Cortez a while back when the Agency needed someone to fly an Operative out of a dicy situation. Cortex knows his trade and likes the fact Agent Brooks will pay him extremely well for any risks involved. Tommy scans the Jungle dense canopy. He realizes trying to spot anything below the thick foliage will be difficult, if not impossible. The only reassurance is the most recent location where the Drug Cartel was last seen. As Tommy is briefly lost in thought, Cortez remarks, "Getting close to the site." The Pilot moves the control column to make the chopper tilt to the right and drop to a lower height - then hovers in the air. Tommy looks below at the open flat field beside the river. The grassy clearing is surrounded by trees, bush and tropical vegetation on three sides. There's enough space for the Chopper to land and the Team to set up Base Camp. Cortez gingerly brings the helicopter down to land on the clear ground. The chopper's rotating blades steadily slow to eventually stop. The Team exit the helicopter and begin to offload and unpack the Mission gear and supplies. Brooks arranged for the Team to have Bivouac Military tents, Army cots, and proper sleeping bags. Tommy and Tasker take the Communication equipment out of the chopper and set up the Coms Link to connect with Agent Brooks back in America. The vast Amazon Rainforest has no Cell Phone Towers like urban areas. In the Jungle, cell phones don't work, you use either high-tech military radio Coms, or rugged portable satellite phones. Roberts and

Morgan carry 3 long bags off to the side, where they unzip each bag and begin to assemble the fold out Klepper Kayaks, the type of Kayaks used by Military. When constructed, Roberts and Morgan place the three Kayaks near the water's edge. Tommy, Eli and Cortez, begin to make Camp and set up the olive-green canvass tents. Three tents - two persons per tent. Just hours before, this same Jungle clearing was bare and void of human life and trappings. Now, the site has Army style tents, a tarpaulin protecting the Coms Radio and military laptop, rugged containers holding food and water supplies, and the long Klepper Kayaks for river navigation. The time goes by quickly and before they know it, the sun has set and night comes to the Amazon. Tommy and Eli have dug a pit in the ground and have a fire going. The Team begins to gather around the fire and talk, while others just stare at the dancing flames. Tommy gets everyone's attention and remarks, "Hey, stop talking. - Listen!" Everyone sits quiet and listens as the Amazon Jungle comes 'Alive' at night with various bird calls, the sounds of monkeys and other animals, and the distant roar of a jungle cat - perhaps a leopard or jaguar. Morgan comments, "The jungle sounds noisy at night!" Tasker remarks, "I wouldn't want to be out there in the dark. You don't know what's gonna bite you!" Roberts turns on his tactical flashlight and chuckles, "That's why we have these babies!" He shines the light across everyone's eyes, and his soldier buddy remarks, "Yah, we need these (thumbs) But they see in the dark!" Tommy grins at the banter and comments, "Copy that!" As the fire begins to die down, Tommy pokes the embers with a stick and remarks, "Better get some sleep - we got a busy day tomorrow!" The Team members nod and everyone goes to their respective tent to settle in for some shut-eye. As sleep descends on the Base Camp, the calls and cries of jungle animals and birds fill the night sky.

Early the next morning, the Recon Team gather near the Kayaks and Tommy unfolds his Map and points out the river system where they're located. With everyone's attention, he divides the group into three 2-Man units, each will have a Kayak to travel the river and explore tributaries. A Ninjan will be with each soldier. Team 1 will be Tommy and Morgan, Team 2 is Tasker and Eli, and Team 3 comprises Roberts and Steve. Cortez will guard the Camp - Forest Monkeys are highly curious, and have been known to rummage through supplies and steal food. Tommy, Tasker, and Roberts, synchronize their watches and each man enters the Base coordinates into their Garmin GPS device which will be used to navigate back to Base Camp. The soldiers produce their Amazon Maps to double check that each Map has the same markings and info. With everything confirmed, the soldiers tuck their Maps into their combat vests, safe and secure. Tommy looks about and announces, "Time to move out!" Each team takes a Kayak to the river's edge, lowers it into the water, then sit down in their seats. With all three kayaks in the water, the Recon Team is ready to go, the Ninjans with their weapons, Tommy, Tasker and Roberts with their military rifles. Team 1 paddles out into the river and heads North, Team 2 takes their Kayak South, and Team 3 launch out going East. Each Team will stay in touch through Radio Coms. The Recon Teams navigate the river system in three directions, looking for any telltale signs of the Cartel's operation - old campsites, garbage litter, smoke from Drug Labs, or Cartel members. The Kayaks allow for stealth and silence, letting the Recon members ply shallow waters right beside the shoreline, enabling them to get really close for covert observation. Tommy and Morgan quietly paddle their Kayak on the water, the only sounds are the jungle creatures around them, and the faint water droplets sliding off their paddles. The Kayak skims the river surface smooth as silk. The seconds become minutes, and the minutes become hours. The 3 Recon Units have been paddling for over 4 hours, exploring the water, riverbanks, eddies, and coves. Nothing. Tommy looks at his watch - it's time to head back to Camp. Morgan and Tommy turn the Kayak around and retrace the meandering route back to their Base. They are the first Unit to arrive. Tommy and Morgan pull their Kayak out of the water and up onto the grass 20 feet from the shore. The sound of water ripples alert their attention, and they turn to see Tasker and Eli paddling toward the shore. Reaching the grassy riverbank, Eli and Tasker pull their Kayak up beside the first Kayak. Soon, Roberts and Steve are paddling along the river and turn in. They exit the watercraft and bring it up beside the other Kayaks. All six men stand in a loose circle, and Tommy asks the big question, "Anyone see anything?" The men shake their heads and Tommy remarks, "Tomorrow's another day. We'll explore further, paddle different streams - They're out there - I know it!" Tasker and Roberts reply, "Copy That!" At that moment, Cortez strides up and proudly declares, "I made some grub! (Scans faces) Who's hungry?" Steve announces, "I'm hungry!", and Eli comments, "You're always hungry." The men chuckle and smile, they're tired and hungry from all the paddling, and ready for something to eat. The Team move toward the tents, and the meal and campfire that Cortez made. Day One Recon is over — no results! The tropical sun has set below the horizon and the Amazon becomes shrouded in darkness, except for the moonlight that peeks through the clouds overhead. As before, the jungle around Base Camp stirs, as animals, birds, insects, make noise with their calls, cries, and sounds of nature. The Recon members cluster around the campfire and eat the hearty stew that Cortez cooked. Appetites are strong from the day's hard work of paddling great distances under the hot sun, where temperatures in the Amazon can reach above double digits. Tommy doesn't have to remind anyone about getting rest - one by one, as the men finish their meal, each person heads for their tent to get a good night's sleep. Only Tommy and Cortez remain sitting by the fire. Tommy stands to his feet and walks over to the Coms Radio set, and reports to Agent Brooks. Over the mesh speaker, Agent Brooks' voice comes across, "Find any sign of the Cartel, Sergeant Long Grass?" Tommy replies, "Negative Sir! The Jungle has many places to hide. Don't worry Agent Brooks, our Team will find them." Brief radio static, then Brooks responds, "The window of opportunity narrows each day! Inside sources tell us the Cartel are halfway through production. After that, they will distribute the deadly drug. We cannot have that!" Tommy answers, "Affirmative Sir! We'll keep searching. Over - Out!" Brooks signs off, "10-4 Sergeant. Good Night!" Now that "Poppa Bear" has been contacted, Tommy closes the Com equipment, and slowly walks back to the campfire. Cortez glances at Tommy and remarks, "Go on Sir! Turn in for the night. I'll put out the fire." Tommy is very tired and happily nods at Cortez's offer. The Recon Leader gets up, stretches, walks over to enter his tent and get some much needed shuteye. Cortez grabs the nearby rifle and brings it beside him, as he watches the fire burn itself out.

The group are up before the sun rises, everyone rested and refreshed - ready for another day of hunting the Drug Cartel. As the Team gather by the Kayaks, Tommy pulls out the Map and calls attention to the river systems they have already covered. The Amazon, being the world's largest and widest river system, has big major rivers that the boats and barges use to carry people, produce, and products, up and down the waterways to the various towns and villages along the river. The obscure rivers the Recon Team are searching belong to the geographic location where the Cartel were seen. This area of the Amazon has numerous tributaries and jungle streams that interlace the

Amazon Rainforest, making the search difficult. As all eyes are fastened to the Map, Tasker points to a section, "Our Team will try there." Tommy nods and replies, "Good.", then he points to another section of the Map, "Roberts, Steve, you both check this area. Roberts comments, "Copy That!". Tommy looks at Morgan, "We'll take the Kayak over here." With new areas to investigate, the three units get into their kayaks and paddle off in separate directions once again. It's still early morning, the day is just beginning, the Team will have ample daylight to hunt the Cartel.

Tommy and Morgan paddle along a jungle creek, the stream seems narrow because of tree branches and thick vegetation hanging over the water at the shoreline. It seems like the two men are enveloped by the jungle itself, as their Kayak floats in the middle of the still waterway. The two put their paddles into the water and silently move the kayak further and further down stream. As they come around a bend, Tommy notices broken branches on the shoreline - signs that humans were here. Animals in nature, do not break branches or snap twigs as the creatures roam, traipse, or even run through their habitat. The only creatures that leave these kinds of signs - are people. Morgan and Tommy bring the Kayak beside the riverbank, as they steady the watercraft, they both exit and pull the Kayak up on the ground. Tommy and Morgan walk to where there are broken branches and twigs. Tommy spots a piece of fabric caught on a broken branch, and he picks it up for closer inspection. Morgan and Tommy study the material - then Tommy remarks, "This is cotton off some type of clothing (Pause) Maybe a sweater, hoodie, or T shirt." Morgan reaches out to handle the fabric and responds, "Tommy, I think you're right. - it's definitely man-made." Tommy scans his eyes to and fro across the ground, and among the trees and vegetation - Behold, he spots boot impressions left on the ground. The boot tracks lead away from the river and into the jungle ahead. Tommy swings his M4A1 military carbine in front, and Morgan pulls out his Eagle Claw batons. The two proceed with care and caution - moving from the small jungle stream into the thick Amazon Rainforest. As they quietly walk among the tropical trees, the treetop canopy blocks out the bright sun, the dense foliage creates a forest interior of dark shadows and narrow shafts of sunlight. Tommy and Morgan move through the shadowy confines going deeper into the jungle, until they stumble upon an old campfire that has evidence of human activity - overturned rocks, tiny chips of chopped wood, and a plastic food wrapper. Morgan examines the fire pit and picks up the food wrapper, "Looks like it's from a candy bar or snack item." Tommy gives the wood chips a flick with the toe of his boot, "Appears they used a small axe or big knife!" Suddenly, crackling in the bushes nearby spook them. Tommy aims his M4A1 and Morgan has the Eagle Claw batons ready for battle. The two men stand with adrenaline pumping through their veins. The two wait in silence - Then, there's a deep growl from the brush 20 feet away - a large spotted jaguar creeps out from under the ferns - the animals big fangs are exposed as it snarls and growls at Tommy and Morgan. Tommy quickly remarks, "We're in it's territory! It feels threatened." Morgan quietly whispers, "Let's back our way out of here!" Tommy with eyes glued on the jaguar in crouch position, "Copy That, brother!" The two men slowly back away from the big jungle cat, being careful not to make any threatening moves. After a number of backward paces, the Jaguar quickly disappears into the thick vegetation. Tommy and Morgan regain their composure and Morgan comments, "That was close!" Tommy grins and replies, "I love animals - but not enough to be their dinner!" They both laugh and retrace their steps back to the Kayak. Tommy gets out the Map and marks their location as a Cartel sighting. Putting the Kayak back into the water, they paddle toward Base Camp, eager to share what they discovered.

At Base Camp, the Team form a huddle as Tommy and Morgan share how they found the broken branches, piece of fabric, boot prints, and the old Campfire. Tasker's Special Forces experience sizes things up quick, he remarks, "Well, I can tell you Amazon Indians don't wear boots, and they don't leave food wrappers behind!" Roberts chimes in, "All of us should head out - go after them!" Tommy looks at his Recon Team and nods, "We'll go after them - as soon as we can resupply our water and gather more ammo. (Pause) Recon - Let's move out!" The group quickly disperse to get fresh water, supplies, and additional ammunition. The Ninjans swiftly ready their weapons and fighting gear - Shuriken stars, poison darts, potions, projectiles, and assorted bombs. When everyone reassembles - the entire group look fierce and battle ready. Tommy, Tasker and Roberts, outfitted with the M4A1, HK416, and the FN SCAR assault rifles, M67 Grenades and the M203 Grenade Launcher. The Ninjans bristle with deadly Ninja weapons - the razor sharp Ninjato and Katana swords, fighting knives, lethal throwing stars, the ferocious Eagle Claws Batons, the formidable Chain

Dart, and pouches containing poisons, powders, and bombs. The Team form a small huddle as Tommy points on the Map where they found the campfire and boot prints. Tasker, Roberts and Tommy enter the GPS coordinates, and each soldier goes to their Kayak, to be joined by their Ninjan partner. When all three Kayaks are in the water, the Recon Team head out toward the location with Tommy in the lead. After a while of steady paddling, Tommy raises his arm to signal to the others they're close to the site. The team paddle in quietly to reach shore and pull the Kayaks up on land. Everyone couches down to be less visible and keep their eyes on Tommy. He waves the Team forward and they move through the Rainforest in stealth mode - treading slow and silent, mindful to not create noise. They reach the abandoned Campsite and keep their eyes peeled for anything - or anyone. Tommy retrieves the Map and examines their present location against the Map details, he whispers, "There is only one direction anyone could go on foot (points) West!" The men lean in to view the Map, and Roberts and Tasker agree, "Copy That, Sergeant!" Tommy stands up from his crouch position, he begins to walk West and his Team follow. Morgan, Eli and Steve carry the rearguard, while Tommy, Tasker and Roberts take point. As the Recon team move deeper and deeper into the Rainforest, the shadowy green interior is both peaceful, yet somehow menacing - one never knows what's behind the next tree, bush or large fern. The tree canopy above their heads allows in shafts of sunlight, letting the men know the sun is bright and strong. The temperature on the Rainforest floor is cooler because of the shade provided from the dense canopy. Morgan and Eli look above to see troops of small monkeys swinging through the trees high above - no doubt very curious about the two-legged creatures walking the forest floor below. The men traverse the ground, the group moves between twisted tree trunks, over thick moss covered rocks, their machetes cutting through the thick brush to create a path forward. Suddenly, Tommy lifts his arm in the air - the signal to Hold. Everyone stops and catches a breather as the Recon leader scopes out the next step. What lays before them is a steep slope that descends at a sharp angle to the fast-flowing river below where large rocks have the swift water swirling and churning. Without Tommy's alert, everyone would have stepped out of the dense vegetation - only to fall forward tumbling down the slope, perhaps to their death in the raging river below. As the Team cluster at the top of the steep incline, they're able to get a panoramic picture of the majestic Rainforest from their high elevation - the view is spectacular! As the men take in the vantage point, Tasker bends his head toward Tommy and remarks, "If we can't go further - Neither did the Cartel! Maybe we missed a trail sign or clue?" Tommy exchanges eye contact and replies, "Let's retrace our steps - see if we missed anything!" Tasker nods. Tommy scans the faces of the Team, "We retrace our steps - keep your eyes open for anything - and I mean anything - whatever catches your attention!" Everyone indicates acknowledgement and the men turn around and set forth to return via the path they cut through the jungle.

The entire Team plod their way back over the route they created - careful to observe the terrain and trail for any clues that were missed. The going is slow. Finally, the Team reach the riverbank from where they initially started. There is frustration in Tommy's eyes, he can't understand why they didn't find more clues or have more success. He looks up at the sky, then glances at his watch, Roberts and Tasker do the same. Tommy comments, "There's enough daylight to make it to Camp. We'll go out tomorrow." Everyone gets into their Kayak and the Team begins to paddle away. Returning to Base Camp, the Team members freshen up, get rested, and look forward to the evening meal. Earlier in the day, Cortez hunted a bush pig, and now has it roasting on a spit over a roaring fire. The hungry Recon Team gather around the roasted pig, and Steve remarks, "Great. BBQ!", that makes the others chuckle. Soon, everyone is 'chowing down' on the delicious savoury pork and sharing conversation around the glowing fire.

The sky is clear and a full moon is out lighting up the night. In the nearby Rainforest, amid the Jungle undergrowth, eyes are cautiously watching the group of men - eyes that don't belong to the jungle animals - these are human eyes, carefully observing, focusing here and there, collecting information with each gaze.

# CHAPTER TWENTY-EIGHT
*The Surprise Encounter*

With the early morning air filled with assorted bird calls, the Recon Team stir to greet the day. Cortez has made coffee and tea, and a supply of biscuits to kick-start appetites. Today's breakfast will be a supply of MREs, the military style "Meals Ready to Eat". As Cortez distributes the sealed foil pouches, Morgan, Eli and Steve, study the package in a wary manner. Morgan remarks to Tommy, "What are these?" Tommy looks at his Ninjan friends and replies, "Meal Ready to Eat" - Soldiers live on these." Eli opens his pouch, looks inside and takes a sniff. Roberts grins, "It's an 'Acquired Taste'!" The Ninjans watch as Tommy and the two Ex-Special Forces soldiers dig into their MRE. Morgan looks at Eli and Steve and comments, "Here goes!", and he begins to eat his MRE. Steve and Eli look for the reaction, and Morgan remarks, "Not bad! Not bad at all." Hearing their friend's assessment, Eli and Steve begin to sample, then fully devour their MRE. Steve glances at Roberts with a smile, "Yes! Definitely an 'Acquired Taste'!" Everyone laughs.

Tommy stands to his feet and begins to walk to his tent, when he spots a group of Amazon Indians standing at the edge of the trees to his right. Tommy cautiously warns the men in a whispered tone, "No sudden moves! Natives. 3 O'Clock." The men turn their eyes toward the dense trees on the right, and see a group of twenty Amazon Indians just standing still, observing them from the edge of the forest. These Amazon Indians are primitive-looking with tribal facial marking, wearing only loincloths, and carry bows and arrows, spears, and long blowpipes. A few of the Indians have colourful feathers tied in their hair, some wear a handmade tribal necklace. The two groups stand motionless and simply stare at each other. Tommy gets Cortez's attention and asks, "From your jungle experience - What do we do?" Cortez adjusts his floppy canvass bush hat and replies, "We wait for them to make a move. They will either disappear back into the jungle - or - they will approach us out of curiosity!" Tommy with his eyes on the Amazon natives remarks, "Copy that!" The scene is surreal with the two groups locked in a staring match, one group dressed in military fatigues, high-tech clothing, carrying military and Ninjan weapons; while the other group clothed in loincloths, have only have simple spears, blowpipes, and bows. The seconds turn into minutes that seem excruciating long - then a break. Five of the Indians begin to step out from their group and walk toward the Recon Team. As the Indians get near, it's plain to see of the five, three are aged men well into their years - likely Tribal Elders. Reaching 30 feet from the Recon Team, the Indians stop and look with expressionless faces - making the situation all the more difficult to read. Cortez glances at Tommy and comments, "Let's you and I take a  few steps toward them - then stop - see how they respond!" Tommy nods and he and Cortez slowly walk to within 15 feet of the Indians, stop and silently stand there. Tommy looks at the faces of the five Amazon Indians, he can feel their eyes examine him from head to foot - their eyes keenly observing, their faces stoic without expression. Tommy thinks to himself they are difficult to read - (what do they want?)(what do we do?). To Tommy and the Recon Team's surprise, the oldest looking Elder speaks in Portuguese, "We saw the shiny sky bird. We watch - why are you in our Jungle?" Cortez quickly glances at Tommy and remarks with a smile, "They speak Portuguese! The old guy likely picked up the language over the years." Cortez replies to the Tribe's Elder in Portuguese with a respectful tone, "We are here looking for bad people. Bad people making drugs that hurt others!" The Elder speaks with the his four comrades in their tribal dialect, translating Cortez's words. Upon receiving the translation, the five Indians look intently at Tommy and Cortez, then the old man comments, "The bad men you speak of came into our lands two rainy seasons ago. (Pause) These bad people killed many of our people." Cortez translates and Tommy looks directly at the Indian Elder and remarks, "Tell them we hunt the same bad people. We cannot find them. Do you know where they are?" Cortez relays the message and the Elder communicates what was said to the others. Lively chatter erupts among the five Indians, which causes a bit of alarm with Tommy and Cortez because they're unaware of how the Indians are reacting. During the Indians' energetic verbal exchange, individual Indians cast glances at Tommy and Cortez as their Tribal discussion continues. Then their chatter stops and the old Indian Elder steps toward Cortez and Tommy to remark, "We know where these bad ones are! We will help you find them - to remove them from our lands - These bad men poison the jungle!" Cortez grins at hearing the old man's message and turns to Tommy with excitement, "They know where the Drug Cartel are! They will help us find them - They want the Cartel out from their jungle." Tommy smiles wide at such great news! He looks at the Indian Elder, smiles and gives the old man a nod. There's a twinkle in the old man's eyes knowing at last, that the Tribe have found help against those who killed tribe members and have polluted their home in the Amazon. The aged Indian Elder looks at Tommy and Cortez and remarks, "Tomorrow, we meet here as the sun rises - We will show you where the Bad people are!" As the Indians turn to leave, Cortez calls out, "Tribal Elder, what is the name of your Tribe?" The old man stops, turns about and replies in Portuguese, "Tribo de Rio Preto!" As the Old man and his four companies walk away, Tommy asks Cortez, "What did you ask him?" Cortez replies, "What's the name of his Tribe?" Tommy enquires, "What did he say?" Cortez smiles and comments, "In Portuguese, They call themselves the "Tribo de Rio Preto - the Black River Tribe!". Cortez, Tommy and the rest of the Recon Team, watch as the five Indians rejoin their group, then they all quickly disappear into the dense jungle.

Later that evening, Tommy is on the Radio Com to Agent Brooks, "Poppa Bear. Poppa Bear Come in. Sergeant Long Grass reporting". Tommy listens with the headset presses against his one ear, "Poppa Bear here. How's the Mission?" Tommy smiles as he replies into the radio mic, "Operation Tomahawk is a Go! An Amazon Indian Tribe will take us to the Cartel. We will Paint Targets as ordered. Copy." There's a bit of radio silence, then Agent Brooks replies, "Copy that, Sergeant! Drones will be ready! I repeat, Drones will be in the sky." Tommy signs off, "10-4 Poppa Bear! Over and Out." Agent Brooks responds, Good Hunting Sergeant!" Tommy turns off the Radio Coms and locks the robust military case shut. He stands up and walks toward his tent. The Recon leader is ready for sleep and tomorrow's 'Big Hunt'!

The next day, as the morning sun rises bright and early, The Recon Team and the Amazon Indian Tribe meet as arranged. Tommy and the others are amazed to see ten dugout canoes filled with the Tribes' warriors armed with bow and arrow, spears, large knives, and blowpipes that shoot poison darts. The Amazon Indians are very curious about the Ninjans. The Indian Elders and warriors gather around the Ninjans to examine and touch the Ninjan clothing and weapons. The Tribe warriors look at Morgans's sharp Eagle Claw batons, and the Ninjato and Katana Swords. They check out Steve's black Chain Dart and the assorted black Shuriken throwing Stars. What really intrigues the Elders and Tribe's warriors is Eli's big black Ninjan Bow and the black leather stealth filled with Black Ninjan arrows. Morgan, Steve, and Eli allow the Elders and warriors to see and touch their Ninjan weapons. The Elders and warriors smile delight at the new experience of handling the Ninjan weapons - the kind of weapons these Amazon Indians have never seen before. When Tommy senses that the time of 'Show-and-Tell' has concluded, he signals and calls out, "Let's move out!" He looks at Cortez and comments, "You're the Team's Interpreter - you go with the Elder!" Cortex nods and communicates with the Elder that he's travelling with them in the dugout. The Elder nods, he understands. With the Elder and Cortez in front, and Tommy and Morgan beside them, the Recon Kayaks and the Tribe dugouts, launch out on to hunt and take down the Drug Cartel.

# CHAPTER TWENTY-NINE
## *The Drug Cartel*

Two years ago, Leaders of the Drug Cartel thought of a way to make their powerful drugs and avoid the Authorities. A trio of diabolical leaders envisioned a drug manufacturing operation without the use of heat, burners, or ovens to 'Cook' the drugs. Instead, the Cartel Bosses thought of mixing special substances and chemicals together to create a new form of street drug, highly addictive and extremely lethal. Just a tiny droplet would be enough to kill a person - man, woman, teenager or child. The Cartel Commanders are cruel, heartless, greedy persons, caring only about the lucrative profits from their drug sales. The problem with previous Drug Labs was that the Authorities would eventually find out the gang's location, and send in Police Forces to stop the operation. One day, as a Cartel leader was relaxing in his luxurious outdoor pool, he watched his glass of liquor sitting in a floating coaster - that's when he got the idea of floating Drug Labs - moveable to evade Authorities, mobile to change their GPS location. The man shared his idea with the other two crime bosses and the evil men embraced the concept as genius. The Cartel bosses planned for all the equipment, supplies, drug labs, sleeping quarters, to be contained on a very large floating platform. Then, one of the bosses became concerned the floating operation could be seen by Authorities. After some deliberation, the Cartel leaders came up with the idea of camouflaging the floating platform to resemble an island - a dense tropical island to blend in with the jungle. This was the inception and the launch of the Cartel's new initiative to use a floating island for their Drug Labs. The Amazon Rainforest was perfect for the Cartel's plan. Not only was the Amazon Rainforest a vast ocean of green vegetation where they could hide the floating island, the Amazon vast river system provided numerous ways to move their Drug Labs around, thus, making it impossible for the Authorities to track and find them. There by the dazzling pool of the palatial Villa, the three Cartel Crime Bosses toasted their new plan to create as many drugs as they wanted, and with no impunity.

The Cartel poured in millions of dollars to create and engineer a very large floating platform covered with expensive landscaping to resemble a tropical jungle island. If seen from above by plane, or from the sides by boat, the entire facility looks realistic - like a jungle island. People say "Money is Power", and the Cartel's stream of money paid for experts to cover the floating platform with tropical trees, large plants, thick bushes, dense vegetation, and tall grass. A military style camouflage netting was constructed to cover and conceal the entire operation. Any plane flying above would look down only to see dense jungle. The Cartel leaders placed big inboard engines that were both powerful and quiet, allowing the floating Drug Labs to be moved on Amazon rivers to various locations. For one period of time, the floating Drug Labs operated in the territory of one country; then, it was moved to a location in a different country. By this means, the Cartel escaped detection and evaded the Authorities. The Amazon Rainforest Cartel focused all their efforts on creating a highly addictive, intensely euphoric, extremely lethal new drug - without the use of ovens, burners or heat - just simply mixing substances and letting the concoction cure a number of days. The greedy Cartel wanted to distribute the new drug across America - enslaving countless addicts - and creating millions of customers to funnel even more money into the Drug Cartel's hands.

Somehow, somewhere, news of the floating Drug Labs was overheard, perhaps at a bar where someone with too much alcohol 'bragged' about working on such an engineering marvel; or maybe a 'Spy' from some rival infiltrated their ranks and took information back. Regardless of the source of the leak, the Secret Government Agency discovered the intel and began a plan to stop the new Drug threat aimed at America. Because the floating Drug Labs were moveable, Brooks and the Agency could not get the exact location of the Drug Cartel. With nowhere to strike, the Secret Agency felt powerless! The ingenious operation made the Drug Cartel Leaders feel 'unbeatable', and they believed their floating island would never be detected, no matter how hard the Authorities or their rivals tried. After all, their camouflaged floating island not only make them 'Invincible', it also makes them 'Invisible'!

# CHAPTER THIRTY
*Operation Tomahawk*

The Amazon Black River Tribe take Tommy and the Recon Team to the region of the Amazon where the Drug Cartel are presently operating. The Recon members and their Indian allies gather in a secluded spot, and the Indian Elder points his finger toward a thick jungle shore up in the distance. Cortez strains his eyes to look and comments to the old man, "I don't see anything but jungle!" The Tribal Elder remarks, "Not jungle - Islands that look like jungle. Bad men on island!" Cortez gives the old man a stunned stare and looks over at Tommy, "The Indian Elder said that jungle shoreline over there is a floating island. He said the Cartel's on it." Tommy stares hard at what looks like a typical jungle riverbank he's paddled by before. The Recon leader ponders a minute than gets Morgan, Eli and Steve's attention - this is the very reason he wanted the Ninjans on the Recon Team. As Eli and Steve paddle close by, Tommy looks at his friends and remarks, "The Indian Elder said the Cartel are on some kind of floating island. (Gestures) Sneak on the island with me and gather Intel. Find out what we're up against." Eli, Steve and Morgan nod. They move to the riverbank to exchange seating. Tasker steps out and gives Steve his seat in the kayak. With everyone set, Tommy and Morgan, Eli and Steve, quietly paddle their kayaks up to the jungle shoreline and move the thick leafy foliage aside - only to reveal to their amazement they are able to set their feet onto big logs fixed together to form a large raft - a large camouflaged floating island. From the outside, one sees only the dense jungle shoreline, but on the floating island itself, one is keenly aware of standing on a man-made structure. Tommy marvels inside at how the floating island appears so real with it's artificial trees, bushes, plants, ferns and tall grass. He looks up to see the entire area covered with camouflaged netting smilier to what the military use. This floating island could perhaps be the envy of a Hollywood Set Designer - the place looks so real, the craftsmanship that good! Crouched down and concealed by leafy foliage, Tommy gives instruction, "We need to find out where the drug labs are, supply sheds, Cartel sleeping quarters, and what firepower we're up against." His three Ninjan friends give firm nods. Tommy gives a signal and all four sneak through the concealed drug making operation. The Ninjans use ancient techniques of Ninja stealth to get close beside buildings, equipment, and supplies. Tommy and the Ninjans later regroup to confer. Morgan remarks, "The Cartel sleep in the buildings at the end. Eli comments, "I found the drug supples in sheds at the other end. Steve adds in, "The Drug Labs are in the centre." Tommy comments, "Great work guys - Valuable Intel. I found out they have four two-man teams carrying AK47s, patrolling and guarding all four directions." At that very moment, Tommy and the Ninjans hear nearby boot steps, they drop low and duck under the thick foliage. As they watch through the openings in the artificial plants, they see two Cartel guards on patrol carrying their AK47s. After a couple minutes, the guards leave. The four Recon members quietly sneak back to their kayaks moored by a thick clump of bushes, get in and paddle back to the group waiting in a nearby cove out of sight.

When the Ninjans and Tommy return to the group, everyone is eager to hear what they found about the floating island. The Team pull their watercraft out of the river and onto shore. They all gather around as Tommy sketches out the Cartel's operation. Tommy draws a rough outline of the artificial island's perimeter, then he draws the buildings, labs, supply sheds, and the four areas where the guards patrol. The Recon leader tells everyone to study the Drug Cartel's layout. Tommy encourages, "Take a good look and make a mental note. The Amazon Tribe and Recon will attack from four directions. The Drug Labs are in the middle (Looks at Tasker & Roberts) We Paint the Drug Labs and supply sheds. Kaboom!" Roberts and Tasker grin and reply, "Copy that Sergeant!" Tommy turns to Cortez, "You will tell the Indians to attack from East and West. Where the sun rises - where the sun sets." Cortez conveys the attack instructions to the Black River Tribe, they nod they understand. Tommy motions Tasker and Roberts to synchronize watches with him to time the attack. He looks at the Recon Team and Amazon Indians - and remarks, "We attack at 1600 hours (eyes Cortez and Ninjans) at 4 PM sharp, we take down the Drug Cartel Operation.

All eyes are on the Recon leader - he waves his hand and orders, "Move out!" The Kayaks and dugout canoes leave the secluded cove and go in their respective locations - and wait for the moment to descend upon the unsuspecting Cartel. Concealed by the thick brush, Tommy, Morgan and eight Indians wait. Across from them is Tasker, Roberts, Eli, Steve, and six Amazon Tribe warriors. With his eyes fixed on his watch, Tommy sees the second hand sweep - 2 minutes - 1 minute - 30 seconds. When the minute hand hits 1600 hours, the four groups launch their Attack on the Cartel Operation! The guard patrols are take totally by surprise and swiftly put out of action. Each attack force moves toward the centre of the large floating island. The Drug Cartel members are shocked and alarmed to see the Recon force and the Amazon Indians attack from all four sides. The gangsters start to fire their automatic weapons, shotguns, and 9mm pistols. Fifty Cartel members fight back sending a deluge of bullets at the Attackers. No matter the Cartel's vain attempt, Tommy's experience in warfare and battle strategy has created a superior position, and the Cartel is trapped in a well-devised "Kill Zone". Tommy, Tasker, and Roberts blast armed thugs with bullets from their assault rifles, the Amazon Indians shoot arrows, spears and poison darts at their enemies; Morgan, Eli and Steve fire Ninjan projectiles, black arrows, and sharp deadly Shuriken stars at Cartel thugs. In the close quarter combat, the Cartel gangsters are decimated as the Ninjans swing their swords, flail the lethal Chain Dart, and strike with the Eagle Claw batons. The Cartel's floating island is littered with gangsters that are unconscious, incapacitated, seriously wounded, or lifeless. The battle is not over as there are still plenty of armed Cartel shooting at the Indians and the Recon Team. Cartel thugs fire their automatic rifles at the Amazon Indians killing a number and wounding others. The shooting back and forth is intense and Roberts gets wounded in his leg. Tommy applies a tourniquet to stop the bleeding and wraps the wound with field dressing. Tommy looks at Roberts and remarks, "You okay?", and Roberts replies, "Affirmative, Sir!" The ex-Special Forces soldier stands to his feet and grips his FN Scar combat rifle and gives Tommy a firm head nod. Tommy and Roberts get back into the action. In the thick of the firefight, Tommy uses the satellite phone to communicate with Agent Brooks, "Going to Paint Targets", to which Brooks replies, "You got three minutes before the Missiles strike - Time to clear out!" Tommy swiftly replies, "Copy that, Poppa Bear! Over-Out!" Tommy, Tasker and Roberts, aim their infrared Lasers at the Drug Labs and

Supply Sheds. Once they hit the targets with the Lasers, the Ex-Special Forces soldiers high tail it out of there. Tommy signals for everyone to evacuate the floating island. Miles away, high up in the sky, the Agency's Drones fire Missiles. When the Lasers hit the Drug Labs and Supply Sheds, the infrared light beams refracted into the air. The sophisticated electronics of the missiles read the infrared beams and the missiles' automatic guidance locked onto the "Painted Targets". In less than a minute, Tommy, the Recon Team and the Amazon Indians swiftly leave the floating island that's doomed for destruction. As Recon members and their Indian allies watch from the safety of the secluded cove - everyone hears the high-pitched SHRILL of incoming missiles - they see and hear numerous EXPLOSIONS as big fireballs rock the jungle. Tommy and everyone look to see the floating island is no longer there - the elusive Amazon Drug Cartel vaporized, the drug manufacturing operation destroyed, the gang obliterated, the once camouflaged island blown to smithereens, whatever little remains is engulfed in flame, soon to vanish from existence.

The Recon members look at Tommy, and Tasker proudly remarks, "You did it, Sergeant! Destroyed the Cartel and the deadly new drug!" Tommy scans the faces of his Recon Team and the Indian allies, and replies, "We did it! We took out the Drug Cartel and stopped the deadly drug getting to America!" Everyone exchanges eye contact and nod their heads. Morgan comments, "Yes! It took all of us - And we had a great Mission Leader!" Roberts and Tasker pipe up, "Copy that. HOORAH!" The task force make their way back to Base Camp, paddling past the burning debris left floating on the river. Reaching the Camp, the Recon Team bid their Indian allies bye and watch as the Tribal Elder and his warriors quietly paddle their dugouts away, going around a bend and out of sight. Tommy eyes his men and comments, "Time to Celebrate!" Some stand and others sit before a roaring bonfire created for the special occasion. Cortez pours everyone some bubbly from a big bottle of Champagne, reserved for such an occasion. Tommy clears his throat and comments, "I like to propose a Toast!" At that point everyone stands with cups or mugs in hand, their eyes fixed on their leader. Tommy slowly looks across the faces of each Recon member, then he remarks, "To Operation Tomahawk and Team Recon!" All the men drink back the toast, smile and bellow in unison, "HOORAH!" Tommy grins that his Ninjan pals have taken to the Military battle cry. Suddenly, Tasker steps forward and declares,

"Cortez. Pour us another Toast." As Cortez takes the bottle to refill the cups and mugs, Tasker looks over at Tommy and remarks, "To Sergeant Tommy Long Grass - a great Mission Leader! A superb Soldier!" Everyone lifts up their beverage holder and drinks back the Toast and loudly yell, "HOORAH!" By now, the Champagne has taken effect and the men are jovial, happy and feeling good. The Team talk and share stories into the late night hours, and they bond as only battle warriors can. It's in the early morning, when everyone retires to get a well-deserved rest from such a grand victorious day!

**OPERATION  TOMAHAWK - A SUCCESS!**

# CHAPTER THIRTY-ONE
*Amazon Friends*

The morning sun has just peeked over the horizon, a new day dawns. The Amazon stirs with the tropical life and vitality as jungle birds, creatures and animals, send forth their cries and calls.

Tommy and the Recon Team are striking Base Camp, when a large group of the Amazon Black River Indians appear at the edge of the jungle. Cortez spots them and alerts the Team members, "Look! Our allies are back." Tommy and the Recon Team stop what they doing and begin to walk toward their visitors. Tribal Elders and warriors walk out from the Rainforest to meet them. There in the middle of the jungle clearing, both groups greet each other with smiles and handshakes. The Elder that joined the Team in attacking the Drug Cartel, steps forward and stands before Tommy. The Elder glances at Cortez and speaks, "You helped us to remove the evil ones from our jungle! Our Tribe want to thank you!" Cortez translates to the Recon Team. The Tribal Elder motions with his hand and some warriors approach the Recon Team and present each member with a large chunk of genuine gold. The old warrior remarks, "We give you the yellow rocks that come from our land!" The Elders and warriors watch with smiles, as Tommy and Team are stunned at the size of the gold pieces. The men grasp the gold rocks with jubilation! They turn the gold chunks in their hands every which way, mesmerized at how the gold glitters and shines. Tommy tells Cortez to express Thanks to the Tribe for their gift of gratitude. As Cortez shares the message that Tommy spoke, The Tribal Elder steps up to Tommy and presents the Recon leader with a Tribal necklace made of coloured beads and Jaguar claws. The old man offers the necklace and Tommy humbly accepts. As the warriors, Elders, and Recon Team look on, the Tribe's Elder asks Cortez to give this message to Tommy, "This Jaguar necklace is our Tribe's great honour given to a great warrior. This honour is yours!" Cortez translates the Elder's words, and Tommy's eyes get moist as emotion fills his soul. He knows this gift is a tremendous honour and one he will always treasure as a reminder of Operation Tomahawk, and the friendship made with the Amazon Black River Tribe. The Elder extends his arm and Tommy shakes the old warrior's hand. Next, the Elders and warriors turn around and walk into the shadows of the Rainforest to disappear from sight. Standing there with their hands still gripping the gold chunks, Tommy remarks, "Time to get the gear and supplies packed away!" The Recon Team resume was they were doing and quickly assemble, pack, and store all the equipment for the helicopter flight out. Roberts, Tasker and Morgan, dismantle the Klepper Kayaks which are engineered to fold up and be stored back in the long carrying bags. Tommy seals up the COMs equipment, while Eli, Steve, and Cortez pack up the tents, poles, and canvass tarps. All the equipment and supplies sit in a large pile on the ground where they camped. Cortez eyes the stuff and comments in a light-hearted manner, "Now, to get all this back into the chopper!" All the other men chuckle, and Tommy remarks, "Don't worry - we'll help you!" The men quickly work together lugging the equipment and supplies over and into the Chopper's cargo hold. Everything is tightly packed and tied secure as not to shift in flight. Tommy takes his seat beside Cortez and the rest of the Team climb in the cargo hold to find a spot. Cortez waits a couple minutes, then yells out, "Everyone buckled in?" Tasker bellows from the back, "All set - Ready to go!" Cortez glances at Tommy, pushes a red console knob and the chopper turbines start up and the big propellers begin to rotate - faster and faster - until the blades are a blur. Cortez pulls the control column back and the chopper lifts up off the ground. As the chopper briefly hovers high in the air, then begins to fly away, the Recon team gaze out at the Amazon jungle where they carried out their Mission. No one will forget what was done here - no one will forget it was 'they' who took down the Drug Cartel, and stopped the deadly drug. None of the Recon Team will ever forget that they were part of - Operation Tomahawk!

# CHAPTER THIRTY-TWO
*Flight To Venture*

Cortez flies the chopper out of the clearing located by the river, and retraces his route back to the crude jungle airstrip where he first met the Recon Team. The veteran Pilot sets the chopper down in exactly the same spot as before, Cortez shuts off the chopper engine and the rotating propellers slow to a stop. Tommy turns to Cortez and shakes the pilot's hand, "We couldn't have done this without you!" Cortez grins and responds, "All part of my job, Sarg!" Tommy gives a firm look and remarks, "Seriously, you were the translator for our Amazon friends - our allies for the Mission!" Cortez humbly nods, "Happy to be able to help! I'm just glad the Drug Cartel was destroyed!" Tommy smiles and salutes, "Copy that, Cortez!" Tommy opens the cockpit door and steps out onto the ground. The Team remove the Mission gear and equipment out of the chopper, and pile the stuff beside the dirt airstrip. The Recon members regroup and stand by the runway and look up at the sky in all directions. Roberts asks aloud, "Anyone see the plane?" The others shake their heads! The men stand beside the jungle runway under the blazing Amazon sun - the temperature is hot! Then, they hear it - at first, a faint buzz, which turns into the steady drone of the big propellors of a cargo plane - a Short C-23 Sherpa cargo plane - the same one that flew them into the Amazon. The men look up in the sky to see the shiny metal object getting closer and closer - the plane's engines clearly being heard across the jungle. The plane circles and descends to land on the rough dirt airstrip, the plane's tires kick up dust as the plane touches down and rolls along the ground. The Cargo plane turns about to reposition for take off, and sits with the engine idle. Tommy and the others swiftly transfer their equipment and gear onto the plane. With everything loaded, the Recon Team get onboard and buckle up. Tommy is the last one into the cargo plane - he turns and gives Cortez a parting wave. The chopper pilot gives a "Thumbs Up" and a hearty wave in return. After Tommy walks into the plane's interior, the Cargo Ramp lifts and locks shut. The engines rev high as the cargo plane speeds down the airstrip - the uneven ground makes for a somewhat bumpy ride. The plane goes faster and faster until - Take Off. The pilots ascend the aircraft at a steep angle to avoid hitting tall trees in the jungle. Inside the cargo hold, Tommy and the Team gaze down at the carpet of green that seems to go on forever. The Pilots point the plane West and flies directly for Columbia, South America. As the Sherpa plane cruises steady at 35,000 feet, the Mission Team settle in for the next 3 hours. Tommy watches the faces of his crew - everyone appears tired and needs rest. Tommy pulls up a photo of Sarah on his cell phone - and stares at his beautiful wife. He leans back and shuts his eyes, as he dreams of being with her once again.

After three hours have passed, the Cargo Pilots announce their arrival at the Columbia Airport that was used before. The C-23 Sherpa Pilots radio the Control Tower requesting permission to land - there is a pause - then Air Traffic Control replies, "Cargo Flight N568 - you are clear to land on Runway 5." The Pilots responds, "Thank you Control Tower! Cargo Flight N568 beginning our approach!" The Shorts C-23 Sherpa cargo plane descends lower and lower until the wheels touch down and the aircraft safely lands on the tarmac runway. Tommy looks through the side window and recognizes the Gulfstream jet parked on a nearby runway. The jet's passenger door is open with the access steps lowered. The cargo plane's engines wind down and the spinning propellers stop. Everyone in the cargo hold unbuckle and get to their feet. The Recon Team grab their Mission gear and equipment, and head for the jet to take them home. Tommy walks with the Ninjans, and Tasker and Roberts follow. Reaching the Executive Jet, the Team climb aboard, and find seating in the large plush leather chairs. The classy interior speaks of refinement and sophistication - the perfect surrounding for the Recon Team to fly home, after taking part in such a rough dangerous Mission in the Amazon Jungle.

Tommy looks around at the Team, everyone is settling in for the 6 hour flight. Tasker opens a Mens Magazine to look at sports cars and power boats, Roberts listens to music on his earbuds, Morgan sits in quiet meditation, Steve is eating a package of peanuts and drinking soda pop, and Eli inspects the string on his black Ninjan Bow. Tommy smiles, leans back to relax, and pulls out his cell phone to text Sarah that they're leaving South America. There's a "Ding" and Tommy reads Sarah's reply text - "Can't wait for you to get home! Hugs & Kisses." Tommy grins to himself and pockets his phone. The high-pitched sound of the Jet's engines alert everyone the plane is about to leave. Air Traffic Control gives the official Clearance for the plane to depart - the powerful jet engines go full throttle - thrusting the jet down the Runway at a blistering speed - the rushing air lifts the wings, the wheels leave the ground - and the aircraft soars upward and climbs steady until it reaches 50,000 feet above sea level. Cruising high above the clouds, Tommy peers out the oval passenger window at the blanket of soft fluffy white clouds. He realizes that time will pass quickly, then, they will be in the skies over America, and soon - he will be back with his lovely wife Sarah in their new home! The sound of snoring begins to fill the passenger cabin, Tommy glances about to see all the guys have dozed off - succumbed to the blissful comfort of the oversized reclinable passenger chairs. Tommy shuts his eyes, and settles in for some welcomed sleep where he can dream once more of his beautiful Sarah.

Hours later, the Jet's cabin chimes sound, and the Seat Belt light flashes, alerting everyone to buckle up as the plane will soon land. The Gulfstream descends to a lower altitude to begin its approach to the rural Fletcher Air Field. The pilots bring the jet in for a smooth landing and taxi the aircraft to where the two black SUVs are parked by the Runway. Agent Brooks and his two Associates are standing outside the lead vehicle, awaiting the Recon Team's return. The Gulfstream steers up beside the parked SUVs, the jet's turbine engines wind down, the side door opens and the passenger steps drop into position. Tommy appears at the side door holding his gear, then quickly descends the steps to the ground. Next, it's Tasker and Morgan, followed by Roberts, Eli, and Steve. Everyone bringing their Mission gear with them. Agent Brooks watches the Recon members approach and gather in front of him. Agent Brooks looks at the group and remarks, "Congratulations men! Operation Tomahawk was a complete success! The Cartel is no more, and the drug threat eliminated! (Pause) Your Government Thanks You!" The Recon Team exchange eye contact with one another. Tommy comments, "We had help from our Amazon Indian friends!" Agent Brooks responds, "Affirmative, Sergeant Long Grass! The Agency will find a way to thank them." Agent Brooks looks at the men and remarks, "You men know "Mum's" the word. You can't talk about this - Understood?" Everyone on the Recon Team firmly nods. Brooks remarks, "Good!" The Agent raises his arm and points to the left, and smiles, "Your Jeep and your Truck are gassed up - ready for the trip home." Agent Brooks and the other two Agents Salute the Recon Team, "Operation Tomahawk - HOORAH!" Tommy and the others smile at the gesture. Tommy turns to Tasker and Roberts to shake their hands, and remarks, "You guys really helped to make the Team! You're both great soldiers!" Tommy raises his arm and Salutes the two Ex-Special Forces soldiers. Tasker comments, "Proud to Serve alongside you anytime, Sergeant!" Tasker and Roberts give a return Salute! The military warriors part, Tasker and Roberts holding their black duffle bags, get into the second SUV. Tommy carries his Mission gear over to the Jeep Rubicon and tosses the stuff into the back seat. Morgan is already seated and waiting. Tommy climbs behind the steering wheel and cranks the engine - Vrrrooomm! He presses the gas pedal and moves his sport utility vehicle across the grass and onto the road toward Venture. Morgan glances over at Tommy and remarks with a big grin, "Sure is good to be back!" They both chuckle as the Jeep sails down the road heading toward home and their loved ones.

# CHAPTER THIRTY-THREE

*Back Home Again*

Tommy and Morgan drive the Jeep over county roads to the Highway that will take them to the Indian Reservation of Venture. Coming down the Highway, the Jeep turns off onto Reservation Road that leads into the Native Indian community. Tommy travels past the local homes, shops, and businesses. He sees the small plaza up on the right, and turns into the parking lot, and drives right up to the front to the Gold Eagle Martial Arts Dojo. Morgan looks over at the young man, "Thanks Tommy! Appreciate you giving me a lift!" Tommy and Morgan, both exit and stand beside the Jeep, Tommy walks over and extends his arm to shake Morgan's hand, "I'm the one that needs to Thank You! When I asked for help - you made yourself available - even when I mentioned there could be danger. (Pause) Thank You very much Morgan for being a member of Operation Tomahawk!" Morgan is visibly moved as he shakes Tommy's hand. (Morgan's mind goes back to the first time he met an awkward teenager named Tommy Long Grass. The Martial Arts Sensi recalls how Tommy began Martial Arts, practiced hard, entered Tournaments, won Trophies, and grew into a fine disciplined teenager.) Tommy notices Morgan's reflective state and comments, "Morgan. Anything wrong?" Morgan smiles at Tommy and remarks, "Nothing's wrong. On the contrary - Everything's right!" Tommy responds, "Good! (Waves) Be seeing you." The man watches as Tommy gets in and drives the Jeep away. Morgan turns about, gets out a key and opens the front door of the Gold Eagle Dojo. He carries his black duffle bag inside and closes the door.

It's late afternoon as Tommy drives the Jeep through the community toward the Highway. He stops at the traffic lights, then signals and turns right to head toward home. Driving past familiar landmarks stirs

Tommy's soul - he's so excited to make it back home and be with Sarah again. Tommy scans the road ahead - there, up on the left, is the gravel driveway that leads to their new house. Tommy turns the steering wheel and rolls onto the driveway. The crunch of the Jeep's big Off-Road tires on the crushed gravel announce his approach - Tommy stops, parks, and gleefully taps the Jeep's horn - Beep! Beep! Suddenly, Sarah appears in the front window, she quickly tosses aside her knitting and dashes to open the front door and run to her love. Tommy swiftly exits and runs toward Sarah. The two Sweethearts - the two newly married - run to hold each other in romantic embrace with passionate kisses. Sarah steps back, takes a good look at Tommy, then remarks with a big smile, "Oh! How I've missed you!" Tommy stands tall and manly as he gazes at Sarah, "You were on my mind the whole time!" Sarah responds, "Oh Tommy! My Sweet Tommy!" And she hugs her man tight like she will never let him go. The two love birds stand and gently sway side to side - enthralled in pure bliss. Tommy lowers his hand to lift up Sarah's chin to look into her eyes, "I'm home now! Let's go inside." Tommy and Sarah walk toward the open front door, hugging each other's side. They enter the house and Tommy turns and closes the door. From inside the house, Sarah's voice is heard outside as she merrily giggles, "Tommy…Tommy - Stop that!" Their playful laughter carries across the property, telling anyone and everyone - Tommy and Sarah are together again!

Having breakfast at the Kitchen table next morning, Tommy's cell phone buzzes. He picks up, "Hello!" Barry, his Boss greets him, "Good Morning Tommy - Welcome back!" The young man politely replies, "Thank you Barry! Good Morning to you too!" Barry continues, "Tommy, I want to say - come back to work when you're ready! Your job is always waiting for you." Tommy comments, "I appreciate that Barry. Thanks!" The Auto Shop owner replies, "Well, I simply called to let you know. (Pause) Bye now!" As the call ends, Tommy sets the cell phone aside on the table top. Sarah walks from the counter to sit opposite her husband, and offers her encouragement, "You've just returned from an important Mission - take some time to rest up - you've earned it! (She cups his hand) We can have some "Us" time - Just you and me!" Tommy smiles at his wife's charming words and her gentle style. He's certainly taken by it and responds, "Ok! I can go back to the Shop next week. (Grins and winks) Let's work on that Baby Room!" Sarah tilts her head with a puzzled expression, "We've done everything the room needs!" Tommy raises his eye brows with a mischievous grin as he repeats, "Let's work on the Baby Room!" The light bulb goes off in Sarah's brain and she laughs, "Oh! Now I see - Let's work on the "Baby" room!" Tommy leans toward her as he pushes the kitchen chair back. Sarah's eyes widen as she flees from the table and gleefully teases, "You have to catch me first!" Sarah dashes out of the kitchen with Tommy chasing her. Tommy laughs as Sarah tries to find safety behind the big sofa, the chairs, coffee table, end tables, and floor lamps. The young couple's joyous play fills the house with a sweetness and romance that newly-weds so abundantly have. After some moments - the house is quiet, perhaps Tommy caught Sarah - or perhaps, they let each other get caught. - Often, that's the way it is for those who are deeply in Love!

A week passes by, and Tommy returns to the Auto Shop. Barry Osprey, the owner, is glad one of his prized mechanics is back on the job again. There's plenty of work to deal with due to the backlog of cars, vans, and trucks, that need repair, tune ups, or parts. Three months pass and Barry gives Tommy as well-deserved raise in his pay-check. Sarah's conscientious and diligent work at the Hospital gets recognized and she receives a promotion - Nursing Shift Supervisor. The new job comes with a nice increase in salary, which Sarah's happy to use in saving for the future. On week nights, the couple stay home sharing each other's company; and on weekends, Tommy and Sarah take the Jeep into the wilderness to get fresh air, and to enjoy for some Off-Roading! The couple grew up in the territory and knew each other as teenagers. The Indian Reservation of Venture, the rugged beauty of the surrounding landscape, and the nearby Town with its shops, businesses, and District High School, …is 'Home' to them. This area is where Tommy and Sarah grew up, went to School, got married, and bought their own house. In Tommy and Sarah's mind and heart - there's no other place in the world they care to be than right here, building their home, and some day - build a family!

Now that the Ninjans have returned home - life goes back to usual. Steve works in his Metal Shop welding parts for a big order from a construction company. Across the community, Morgan meets with parents and new students at his Gold Eagle Martial Arts Dojo. Out of town, at the Canyon Run Ranch, Eli watches from the Coral fence as a young man breaks in a new mount. The Rancher figures why take the chance to break old bones, when there's a hired ranch hand available to ride a feisty unbroken horse. And, out on Plains Road, Carl basks in the sun as he sits on the cement front stoop, reading his Travel Book on Japan.

One afternoon, after Tommy and Sarah share a cosy time relaxing on the sofa. Tommy gives Sarah a smile as he phones his Grandpa. Carl sees his grandson is calling and answers, "Hi Tommy - What's up?" Tommy greets Carl, "Hi Grandpa! I was wondering if you can arrange another meeting with the Ninjans?" Carl chuckles and replies, "Last time I set up a meeting - guys ended up halfway around the world!" Tommy quickly assures, "Don't worry! There's no Mission or Travel involved!" Carl replies with encouragement in his voice, "In that case - I'll see what I can do!" Tommy expresses his gratitude, "Thanks Grandpa! Hope to see you soon. Bye." The call ends and Carl tucks the phone into his jean pocket, adjusts his bifocals, and flips through the book to the page where he was reading.

All the Ninjans agree to see Tommy again, and the meeting is set for Carl's brick bungalow on Plains Road, at 7 pm this Friday evening. Tommy motors the Jeep along Plains Road until he comes to that familiar Mail Box - LONG GRASS. The young man steers into the long driveway and sees the guys' vehicles parked on the grass. Tommy pulls the Jeep up under the big Oak tree, the place where he always parked as a teenager while he lived with his Grandparents. He exits the Jeep and walks up the steps and Knocks. Carl yells, "Tommy, you don't have to knock - Come in!" Tommy enters the house and notices the Ninjans sitting around the room. Carl approaches and comments, "Everyone's here! (Pause) I cooked food. Do you want to eat - then have your talk?" Tommy looks at the guys, gives a nod, then comments, "Sure! Let's eat first - then have our talk!" Carl smiles and replies, "Excellent! I made my famous Southwest Nachos!" Carl turns toward the group, "Before Tommy talks with us - I got lots of food - Nachos, Pizza, Hamburgers, Hotdogs, Spicy Chicken Wings, and Pulled Pork-on-a-Bun." Steve injects an offer, "Carl, I'll help bring in the food!" Morgan chimes, "You're only helping so you can get to the food first!" The other guys bust out laughing, and Steve tries to defend his honour, " Just so you know - I grabbed something in town to eat!" Eli teases, "Hope it wasn't someone I know!" Steve curls his face into a frown. Carl puts a gentle hand on Steve's shoulder and remarks,

"Don't be angry with them, Steve. It's just that - everyone knows you're always hungry!" Steve playfully tussles with Carl and Tommy grins and warns Steve, "Don't Steve (eyes Carl) It's his house!" Steve grins and lets go of Carl's arm. At that, all the guys have a laugh as they start to gather at the large dining table. It only takes a couple minutes, before Carl, Tommy, and Steve, quickly cart out the trays of tasty cuisine. With the dining table laden with delicious food, everyone digs in to load their plates with the kind of food hungry men love!  The guys eat and share jokes and conversation like the old friends they are. The food is so good that some of the men have 'seconds', and even 'thirds,' - the trays sit bare and empty, all the food eaten with appreciation.

Now that the food portion of the evening is over - Carl motions for the guys to sit and relax - ready for Tommy to share.  Tommy stands up and clears his throat. The Grandfather realizes what his grandson has to say is important, so Carl comments, "Listen up guys! Tommy's got something to say!" The young man looks across the room at the faces of men he knows and respects. Morgan remarks, "Go ahead Tommy - What's this meeting all about?" The young man reaches out to place his hand on Carl's shoulder, as his Grandpa sits in his favourite chair. Tommy looks with a serious face and remarks, "I've known you men for a long time - since being a kid. You've always been good friends to my Grandpa - and you feel like family. (Looks at guys) That's why I've asked you all to meet with me." Carl and the men are quiet as they listen. Tommy continues, "The reason I've asked you to be here tonight - is - (Tommy breaks into a  great Big Smile) - Sarah and I are going to have baby! - I wanted to personally tell you the good news!" The room erupts with gladness and loud Cheers! The men get up and Congratulate Tommy with hearty handshakes and manly pats on the back. Carl grins and eyes Tommy, "Now, I know why you wanted the meeting!" The Grandfather stands to his feet and proudly shakes his grandson's hand, "Congratulations Tommy! I'm so happy for you and Sarah." An atmosphere of joy and happiness fills the room. All the guys are throughly excited about the arrival of a new baby!

# CHAPTER THIRTY-FOUR
*It's Time!*

Six months later ... Sarah is lovely as ever - and every bit the expectant mother, with her protruding tummy, heavier breasts, midnight cravings, 30 pounds of chubby weight gain, sleepless nights, and accompanying mood swings. Tommy tries his best to be loving and supportive. Sarah has tears and tells Tommy, "I look terrible! Look at me - I'm a whale!" Tommy responds, "Honey, you look great - You're glowing like a soon-to-be-mommy!" Sarah moans, "I'm not glowing - I'm sweating!" Tommy tries a quick recovery, "Sweetheart, to me - you look wonderful at any time." He gives a reassuring hug and peck on her cheek. Sarah glances at her hubby and realizes he's trying his best - after all, the pregnancy hasn't been easy on him either. He's had to miss work at the Garage, make "false emergency' runs to the Hospital, and had his share of sleeping on the sofa, so Sarah can sprawl out trying to cool down to sleep. She gives her darling a sweet smile and reaches out to bring him near, "I'm sorry for snapping at you!" Tommy understands Sarah's struggle and softly replies, "That's ok babe! You were just feeling a little down." Sarah reaches out to hug Tommy close, "Come here, handsome! How about a big ole kiss!" Tommy's kiss takes away Sarah's sadness and energizes her soul. The young woman shifts forward on the sofa, wanting to stand to her feet. She places her left hand on the sofa seat, her right hand grips the sofa arm for support, and she begins her attempt to get off the couch. Tommy quickly gets up and extends his hand to Sarah, "My Lady. May I help you to your feet!" Sarah relies in a light-hearted manner, "Thank You my shining Knight!" Tommy pulls Sarah to her feet with ease. She looks at him with a slight wince, "It's uncomfortable with the baby pressing on my bladder - I really need the bathroom!", Sarah immediately goes into the washroom and shuts the door.

* * *

In was 11:00 pm on a Wednesday night, three weeks later, when Sarah loudly calls out, "Tommy! Tommy! It's Time!" Tommy races up the stairs, and rushes to the bedside, his eyes wide with excitement as he asks, "It's Time?" Sarah smiles and nods, "Yes Hon! My water broke - the baby is on the way!" Tommy helps Sarah out of bed, and she puts on the loose clothing that she especially set aside for this moment. Tommy guides Sarah down the stairs where she briefly stands as Tommy grabs his jacket and car keys. The couple are out the door and in the vehicle. As Tommy drives the Jeep to the Hospital, Sarah groans - the contractions have started! Tommy rushes toward the hospital - glancing over at Sarah as she grimaces from the pain of the contractions. Tommy encourages, "We'll be there soon, Honey!" Sarah groans again as she holds onto the door handle. In a matter of minutes, the Jeep pulls in front of the Hospital steps. Tommy parks, cuts the engine, exits and races up the steps to go inside. A minute later, a Nurse and an Orderly pushing a wheelchair appear at the top of the steps. Tommy quickly descends, opens the passenger door and supports Sarah as she gingerly climbs the Entrance steps. When she reaches the top, the Nurse seats Sarah in the wheelchair, then the Orderly and the Nurse take Sarah directly to a Hospital Delivery Room. Tommy follows close by, keeping his eyes on Sarah at all times. The Staff wheel Sarah into the Delivery Room and transfer her to the hospital bed prepped with big medical sheets. As Sarah reclines with her legs wide apart, a Doctor and another nurse enter the room and come up to the bed. Sarah strains with the contractions, and lifts her eyes to see the Doctor and two Nurses staring up her open smock. Sarah's dealing with the pain, so she doesn't have time to be embarrassed that three strangers are inspecting her private region. As the medical staff do their work to prep Sarah, Tommy stands in the background and offers his wife emotional support and encouraging smiles, letting her know she's not alone - her husband is there with her. The Nurses have hooked up the medical monitors and the Doctor times the contractions - waiting for the baby to arrive. Sarah screams - the contractions are strong and close together. The Doctor looks at Sarah and prompts her, "Push! Push!" Sarah is breathing rapidly, she's soaked with perspiration, her hair is wet and matted, and she feels the contractions from head to toe. The Doctor looks at her Cervix and comments, "I see the head - the baby is Crowning! (To Sarah) Push Again. Push Harder!" Tommy stares as Sarah's body arches and she screams and pushes harder - again and again! The Doctor's voice carries excitement, "The baby is out!" The Doctor picks up the baby and cradles the newborn is a warm clean delivery blanket, inspecting and checking the newborn's face, hands, feet, and body. The Nurses help to clean up Sarah from the messy delivery. Sarah is laying flat, catching her breath - Tommy hasn't taken his eyes off the baby for a nanosecond. As the young couple look at the Physician holding the newborn, the Doctor looks at Sarah and Tommy, "You have a healthy baby boy!" Tommy and Sarah's face light up with exuberant joy and the young couple break out with big smiles. Matter a fact, smiles are all around the room, as the two Nurses and Doctor smile they're able to share the happiness of the baby's safe arrival. The Nurse brings the baby boy and lays the ever so tiny infant in Sarah's arms. Tommy comes over and crouches down close to mother and baby. The moment is sublime, the picture is perfect! Days before, Tommy and Sarah were just a sweet couple; now, with the tiny newborn laying peacefully between mommy and daddy - they're no longer just a couple - from this moment on, Tommy, Sarah, and Baby are a Family!

Since Sarah is a healthy young woman, the Doctor discharges her in the late afternoon with his blessing and best wishes. The new dad pushes the wheelchair toward the Front Entrance as Sarah sits carefully holding their new bundle of joy. Tommy sets the wheelchair with mom and baby off to the side, out of the way of pedestrian traffic, then he goes to bring up the Mustang to the base of the entrance steps. He carefully assists Sarah and the baby down the steps and into the car. The ex-military man had anticipated and planned for this day, the Mustang now features a baby car seat fixed and anchored in the vehicle's back seat. Sarah tenderly puts her baby into the protection of the car seat and baby harness, then lays a small nursery blanket across the infant car seat to help keep the baby warm and block any drafts. The young lady slowly climbs into the back seat to sit beside her newborn. Tommy closes the passenger door, goes over to his side, gets in and starts the Mustang - Vroom! He shifts from park and leaves the parking lot to take the highway back to their house out of town. When they reach home, Tommy helps Sarah and baby into the house and up to the stairs to the second floor. Sarah and Tommy enter the Baby Room and tenderly lay their new baby boy in the comfort and safety of the crib. As Sarah stares at her precious infant son, Tommy makes sure the crib's side rails are locked secure. Sarah smiles at her hubby's good intentions, and touches his hand to remark, "Sweetheart, don't worry about that - babies don't roll around until four to six months!" Tommy grins as he replies, "Oh, I didn't know that! (Looks at son) There's so much to learn about a baby!" Sarah presses in to hug Tommy and comments, "Well, there's tons of books, online videos - and experienced parents we can talk to (nods head) There's lots of help available these days!" Tommy can't take his eyes on his newborn son - he just stares at the little guy wrapped up snug in the baby blanket. Sarah walks over to the Baby Dresser and switches on a charming Carousel baby light that plays gentle nursery music. She takes Tommy's hand and comments, "The baby will be here in the morning - let's get some sleep - I'm so tired!" Tommy puts his arm over Sarah's shoulder as the young parents go to their bedroom. Tommy takes off his shirt as Sarah climbs in on her side. He turns around to tell her something - and he hears faint snoring - Sarah, the young mom who just gave birth - has fallen asleep!

Over the coming days, weeks, and months, Tommy and Sarah are very busy - feeding the baby, changing diapers, holding the baby, watching the baby sleep, - then, it's a continuous repeat of the same. This pattern with babies is something parents of newborns know all too well! And sleep, who gets to sleep - not Sarah or Tommy - they're up at all hours of the night caring for their little one. Tommy was so exhausted, one time he dosed off for a minute at the shop - the loud sound of an airgun snapped him back awake. Sarah has Maternity Leave and spends time preparing the house for the "pitter patter" of little feet. She baby-proofs each room, fitting Safety Plugs in all the outlets, and installing a Baby Rail at the top and bottom of the stairs. As a new mother, Sarah delights in decorating the entire house to announce - this home has a baby! Framed family photos line the walls, adorable plush stuffed toys guard the sofa and chairs, and a beautiful ceramic Noah's Ark with Animals sits on a living room shelf. The kitchen has a sterilizer, baby bottles, and small glass jars of baby food. Yes, if anyone hadn't noticed - a baby lives here! It's taken a long time for Tommy and Sarah to settle on names for their baby boy. The new dad and mom have decided to name their son - **James Thomas Carl Long Grass** - Thomas in honour of dad Tommy, and Carl in honour of the child's Great Grandfather.

As the baby's first Birthday approaches, the couple's family and friends are invited for a big Celebration - a time of Thanksgiving and Blessing! It's a time to be rejoice with the important people in Tommy, Sarah, and little Jamie's life - Sarah's mom and dad, Nana and Poppa Chisholm, Grandpa Carl, The Ninjans, Sarah's friends and coworkers, Tommy's high school friends, and guys from the Auto Shop. Sarah, her mom and some ladies have looked after all the food, and Sarah's dad and Carl arranged for all the beverages and snacks. The day before the "Big Day", Sarah and Tommy decorate the house with party streamers, festive ribbons, colourful helium balloons, and their tiny son's very first Birthday Present. When the day arrives, there are cars, vans, trucks, SUVs, and motorcycles, parked everywhere on the property. The front entrance is decorated with different shades of blue balloons, and party ribbons hang from the house and property trees. Anyone driving by would get the message - There's a big party going on! Inside the modest two story house, people fill the place, standing around, seated on furniture, lining the stairs, even sitting on the floor. Tommy and Sarah are mingling and greeting everyone, thanking them for attending the special occasion! The young parents receive enthusiastic handshakes, endearing hugs, and lots of friendly backslapping. In the kitchen, there's a ton of food - BBQ Chicken, Grilled Hamburgers and Hotdogs, French Fries, Cobs of Corn, Spaghetti, Noodle Casserole, Meat Loaf, Assorted Meat Subs, and Spicy Nachos. The beverages include - Coca Cola, Pepsi, Schweppes Ginger Ale, A&W Root Beer, Low Calorie Coolers, Beer, Lemonade, and Bottled water. The new dad glances over at Carl and nods, then Tommy speaks loud enough to be heard about the lively conversations, "If I could have everybody's attention!" The room quickly becomes quiet and everyone listens. He reaches out to Sarah, the young couple hold hands as they stand in the middle the room. Tommy motions to Carl, "Before we taste all this wonderful food - I want my Grandpa Carl to say the Grace." With everyone's eyes closed, and people being quiet, Carl begins his prayer, "Dear Heavenly Father, Thank You for this very special day! A momentous day, where family and friends join with Tommy and Sarah in Celebrating the little Jamie's First Birthday! The Bible tells us that children are a gift from God! Thank You for precious Jamie being in Sarah and Tommy's life - Please help and guide them to be good and wise parents. Dear Lord, Thank You for all this incredible food, bless the hands that have prepared it. For all this food, Sarah, Tommy, and baby Jamie, - we ask Your Heavenly Blessing

- in Jesus' Name. Amen!" As Carl closes in prayer, all the people begin to stir and move toward the kitchen. Nana Chisholm and her friends have organized the food, setting the trays on the large table, the kitchen countertops, and a folding table brought in to add extra space. The beverages have been set up in the back room where there are plenty of paper cups for thirty souls. The people move from selecting their food items in the kitchen, to getting their drinks in the backroom. Once you get your plate of food and drink, you go through the hall beside the stairs, and back into the living room. All throughout the house, the people are festive and jovial; loving the food, enjoying company, and very happy to take part in the baby's first Birthday. As the friends and family sit eating and sharing conversations, Sarah and Tommy take tiny Jamie around to let the folks see him. The hearts of the ladies melt and the guys smile with pride when they see the little guy. "How Sweet", "Adorable", So Fine", "Beautiful Baby"  are the remarks that Sarah and Tommy hear as others see their baby boy. After a while, Nana Chisholm waves to get her daughter's attention, Sarah nods and grabs Tommy's hand, and the trio walk to stand to the centre of the room. Nana Chisholm and the ladies walk from the kitchen into the packed living room carrying a fantastic Birthday Cake especially decorated for a little boy - Frosted Baby Blue Icing, decorated with an adorable Fire Truck, Police Car, and Cute SUV. One tall solitary candle burns bright in the middle of the cake. Nana Chisholm, ladies and everyone present break forth singing the beloved song known around the world - "Happy Birthday to You! Happy Birthday Dear Jamie!" The eyes of the baby Jamie sparkle and shine as he watches the dancing flame on his first Birthday candle. Nana Chisholm presents the cake to Sarah, Tommy and baby, as everyone keeps singing - Sarah, Tommy, and Jamie, blow out the candle. Everyone CHEERS and claps in happy Celebration!

With everyone having their fill of food, beverages and Birthday cake, Grandpa Carl comes over to Tommy and Sarah, smiles and asks, "Do you think I can take Jamie for a while?" Sarah holds out her tiny son for Carl to hold and cradle. The elderly man with a big smile, walks away carrying his great grandson. At this stage, some people have moved from the house to go outside to get some fresh air and enjoy the pleasant temperature. Grandpa Carl carries little Jamie over to where the Ninjans stand sharing some conversation. Carl approaches them sporting a wide smile, "Guys, I haven't officially introduced my Great

Grandson to you!" The Ninjans stop talking and look at Carl and softly eye at the little boy. Carl carefully supports baby Jamie with one arm, as he points to each of his Ninja friends, "Little Jamie, I want to introduce you to - your Uncle Morgan - your Uncle Eli - your Uncle Steve - and your Uncle Barry!" Jamie's eyes are bright and alert as the tiny tot stares at the faces of the men before him. The Ninjans begin to faun over him as only "Uncles" can do. There's a tender spirit in their midst, their hearts greatly touched by Carl's special gesture. All the Ninjans proudly gaze at their new nephew!

# CHAPTER THIRTY-FIVE
*The Next Generation*

The weekend sun is warm and inviting, coaxing people to be outside to enjoy the outdoors, and bask in the golden rays of the sun. Grandpa Carl is on the home's front porch, sitting in a rocking chair as he lovingly holds his great grandson. Baby Jamie is fussy and hungry and cries - Sarah seated on the living room sofa, hears Jamie's cries and puts aside her knitting, and comes up to Carl. The mommy knows her baby and kindly comments, "Thanks Carl! I'll take little Jamie now - He's got some gripe and is fussy today." Carl holds up the baby, and Sarah takes her child and goes back into the house. As Carl quietly rocks back and forth - watching the birds flutter about in the nearby trees, Tommy approaches and remarks, "Want to practice?" Carl's eyes light up and he merrily replies, "Thought you'd never ask - being so busy as a new dad!" Tommy grins and comments with a wave, "Let's go! We can practice in the back." Carl gets to his feet and walks with Tommy around to the back of the house. Tommy has two sheathed Katana swords laying on top the wooden picnic table. The young man grabs the lacquered black Katana and tosses it Carl. The fit Grandfather catches the black weapon and pulls out the sharp metal sword. Tommy picks up the lacquered red Katana and extends the sword from the scabbard - the sharp blade gleams in the sunlight. The men step away from the picnic table, and walk to a clearing 30 feet from the house. As both grip their sword handle, Tommy bows to Carl, and Carl bows to Tommy. The young man begins to pace side to side, and remarks, "Didn't have much time to practice in the Army - busy and all! (Looks at Katana) I'm likely rusty!" Carl masterly slices the black Katana, and comments, "You likely need practice (swings blade) That's why I'm here!" Tommy grins and calls out, "Let's do this!" Carl replies, "Bring it Grandson!" Sarah holds little Jamie and smiles as she watches from the kitchen window. Both Ninjan Masters launch out against the other with a flurry of swings, blocks, chops, slices, and deflections. Tommy and Carl's Ninja swords are quick flashes of shiny steel locked in Martial Arts combat. Tommy still remembers his skills and technique, but he has slowed from the lack of practice. The young man can field strip a M4A1 assault rifle, plan the Arc of Fire against enemy position, and parachute in the dark of night - but Tommy's technique with the Katana has weakened. Carl repeatedly out-battles and out-maneuvers the young buck, and eventually knocks the red Katana out of Tommy's grip. The old Ninjan Master points the sword blade at Tommy and remarks with a grin, "You sword skills are sorely lacking - But you'll improve - after all, I'm still your Sensi!" Tommy smiles and humbly bows, "Arigato Grandpa! You will always be my Sensi!" Tommy picks his red Katana off the ground, puts the sword back in its scabbard, then extends his hand, "Let's go inside for a coffee, Grandpa. I think Sarah has some pie and ice cream!" Carl grins wide and his eyes twinkle, "Pie and Ice Cream - every Ninjan's weakness!" Grandson and Grandfather laugh as they both go indoors, to once again be with Sarah and little Jamie, - the baby boy who will one day be their **fourth generation - Ninjan**!

**THE END**

www.ingramcontent.com/pod-product-compliance
Lightning Source LLC
Chambersburg PA
CBHW030754200726
48288CB00004B/1174